I0690743

For my children Aidan, Amelia, and Avery

I had no ambition to write before you. And to my husband
Ryan that gave me the time and encouragement over these
30 some years.

Thank you to all those that have helped during the 15 years it took to write and finally publish this book. All of those in my writing group, family, and friends in particular:

Helen Sprinkle, Erin Kollar,
Laura Smith, Christine Laforet, Gretchen Frick Woods,
Chris Gurnick, Chantal Ostroske, Michelle Watt,
Amanda Farrenholz, Jennifer Matlak Cirincione,
Barb Wysocki, and Christian Zimmerman.

Soul Shifters is a work of fiction. Characters, places, events, and names are the product of this author's imagination. Any resemblance to other events, other locations, or other persons, living or dead, is coincidental.

Copyright © 2023 Soul Shifters, by Michelle Kollar

The author reserves all rights to be recognized as the owner of this work. You may not sell or reproduce any part of this book without written consent from the copyright owner.

First paperback edition November 2023

Book design, illustration and publishing setup by: "Me Hand!" Art, Books, & Comics, trademarked and protected by Me Hand LLC, owned and operated by Michelle Kollar.

ISBN 979–8–9895099-0-4 (paperback edition)

# SOUL SHIFTERS

# CHAPTER 01

I'd been taught to fear the stars…

Looking up, there they were in all their deceptive beauty. My parents got to enjoy their magnificence. It wasn't fair. Everyone knew stars equaled death now.

My bloodied fingers stuck to the wheel as I repositioned them. The floor of the boat began to puddle in red, signaling me I was running out of time. I wiped my nose trying to stop the stream of blood from running into my mouth, which felt like it held the current of a faucet.

I don't want to die. I'm not going to die. I'm going to focus and do what Dad told me to do, I thought, wiping more blood from my nose, my hands stained. The wet hem of my cotton dress dripped onto my shoes.

Crying blood and groaning the last mile, I could feel my eyes darkening. Shutting the engine off, something clanged behind me, the keys I supposed, jingling in the ignition as I whipped around. I tied a life jacket around my wrist and jumped in the lake's soothing cold water.

Immediately, everything stopped and there was silence. Every time I came up for air, the searing pain came back again. I fell into a dream state while I gasped and yelled for my dad.

Being five years old the last time this happened, my father drove me to the lake and threw my convulsing feverish body miles from shore. I'm not sure how he knew what to do but the water barred the energies from entering me.

The searing pain dissolved and my body relaxed. There wasn't blood last time. This time, the blood was new, and it was all over the boat.

After a while, I was able to float and stare up at the starry sky. Then the clouds moved and I saw the moon and its path in the water. It was when the sun began to rise that the drones returned.

The drones were unmanned spaceships programmed to hover above our area, and they normally overpowered the starlight. The had left our state to attack vulnerabilities in the protection fields. If one could get in, then many would follow and fight to try. They would cluster, leaving our skies until the breach was fixed, which meant Cleveland was honored with the night sky while a far away city burned to the ground.

Shivering, the air stung my arms leaving them bumpy, and it occurred to me that I could go home now. During the night, the boat had drifted a couple miles further out. I restarted it and headed back, prepared for the consequences.

The closer I came to shore, my heartbeat punched heavier and faster with every pacing second. About a mile from shore, I could make out the beach and knew the police would hide and wait for my return. I would be charged for stargazing because there was no other motive to commit such a crime during a drone attack than that. And I'd done most of it in ravaging pain.

I was tempted to turn off the engine the last half-mile. I rejected my fears even when I saw someone standing on the dock. I took a deep breath and pulled it in. I couldn't make eye contact. I just stared at his shoes. My heart shifted into a higher gear. There was nowhere to run.

Throwing him the line part for him to tie and part to distract, I instinctively hurtled out of the boat and began to run down the dock.

When I reached the top of the landing with no railing,

I noticed he hadn't ran after me. He was on the boat looking at the blood.

The blond-haired guy was dressed in a grey sweatshirt and jeans. He cupped his hands around his mouth trying to magnify the sound. I heard him loud and clear by the echo off the bluffs behind me.

"I know what you are and I can help you," he called up to me. What I was, was a thief and I didn't want his help. His help involved jail. No way was I going to wait around for him to change his mind about calling the police.

# CHAPTER 02

The baker wore his white suit, while waiting at the door. He had fifteen crates today for the party, as opposed to the daily half of one. He smiled kindly, but tapped his toe while waiting for my mother.

"So Don...while you're waiting...What made you decide bakery and delivery for your vocation?" I made conversation.

"I don't know exactly. I wanted a job and found myself in the bakery district. They welcomed me with open arms like I was meant to be there. You're turning eighteen soon, huh?"

"In a few months."

He began to say, "I wouldn't worry too much-

But my mother cut him off with, "Delia, you aren't going to be in baking and delivery. Don't be ridiculous. Your father was a scientist. You'll follow the sciences with school, of course. Bakers don't need schooling, as you call it. Right Don?" Mom glared and smiled at the same time.

"I'm going to need the last name list of everyone attending the party and their addresses, Ma'am," he said to my mother in a professional tone.

"Yes, yes here it is." Mom paid for the food and gave him the names of everyone that would be attending the party.

"Extra rations need to have a reason. I'm sorry, rules are rules.

"I know what the rules are, Don. Honestly, you act like no one has parties." My mother sneered. "Delia, get your butt back to straightening those rooms. We have two hours."

"Don, hold on a second."

"Yes." His smile was wiped away by my mother's comment.

"I'm sorry about my mom, Don. She's just... well, I'm sorry," I sighed.

"Miss Dee, whatever is in your future, I'm glad there are high-class people like you out there. You're different. Gotta go, hun."

Everyone started to arrive. The weeks following the attack, my condition worsened. Before, I could go to school and have friends with no problems. With the country in mourning, I could only handle two to three people in a room at a time without getting a headache. Also, I had no filter. Every thought in my head came straight out of my mouth.

Every day I changed more and more. I became angrier and distant. The few friends I had in school didn't want to hang out, which was fine with me, because their drama gave me migraines.

Then today, Mom decided to have another party. For no reason, she invited everyone we knew to 'come on over' even though she knew how awkward I made situations lately. I'd say something stupid, get a look of disdain, and then get yelled at. Maybe she wanted to snap me out of my funk, but isolation was easier, painless.

"Delia, come over here and look at this picture of you and Great Aunt Helen," someone called out to me after everybody in the entire world arrived.

*Oh yes, can we please look at dead relatives?* I thought.

That one in particular was a great choice. A few days before her death, Great Aunt Helen told me not to be sad about her upcoming passing because she was going to visit me and we'd play games together. You can't tell a three year old that. They will take it literally. I used to have this nightmare about Great Aunt Helen's zombie making me play tether ball with her. Of course, her head had to be the ball.

"She was one crazy old lady," I mumbled, remembering other weirdo stuff she'd whisper to me when my mother's head was turned. She often talked about my future and how very special I was. In my opinion, she was the *special* one.

"What did you say?" asked my Uncle Sean.

"Oh, I was just thinking of the old days," I responded. *Congratulations, you just entered yourself into a conversation*, I scolded myself.

"Yes, they were so long ago," he winked. "You know, when you were a tiny thing, you had the best imagination. Hey Sheila, what was the name of her friend?"

"Which one?" My mother looked up from the photos.

"You know...the one who liked to introduce her to all the walls in the house," he said. The one thing Uncle Sean knew how to do was push his sister's buttons.

"Huh?" And as usual, I wasn't getting his humor.

"We don't talk about her. By the way where is your ear clip?" my mom asked, with her nostrils flared. Her words slapped my face the way they always did.

"Mom, what are you freaking about?" I knew I should stop, but my curiosity was in overdrive. Besides, I needed to distract her from the ear clip. I hadn't seen it since the night of the drone attacks when we lost the city of Houston.

"Which friend was this?" I kept the conversation going. It had been awhile since I had anyone over.

"You need it for school, Delia, and I like knowing where you are at all times. I can't let this go any longer." Mom wouldn't get off it.

"Your imaginary one," Uncle Sean's smile was victorious at her irritation and I was relieved he was unknowingly helping me.

"I had an imaginary friend? What was her name?"

"Ariel," he laughed at my mother's fury. "You followed her everywhere. You even got yourself lost at Cedar Point once because she wanted to see the gift shop instead of going to the bathroom with everyone else."

My mother said through stiff lips, "You were gone for a whole hour. I thought you were kidnapped. And you know that scar above your eyebrow?" She pointed a finger at my forehead with an irate wave, "You got that running into my bookshelf following her into yet another wall. After ten stitches, we said goodbye to Ariel. I think that is enough about her." She stomped away.

Okay, here is the play by play:

Did I talk? Check.

Was my mother in some pissy mood? Check.

Did I get yelled at in front of everyone?

You bet your ass.

I pulled myself away from her irritation to that numb place. It really didn't take much to set her off since my dad died, especially if it involved anything freaky or supernatural.

I sat there held by a sudden flood of memories. The little girl that could walk through walls…could she have been Great Aunt Helen?

I was connecting the dots of every hunch and inkling my mother had gotten so mad at me for over the years. I remembered it was that little girl named Ariel who would tell me things. When I relayed these conversations to my mother, I was always punished, especially when I was right. I never knew why; I just thought she was trying to teach me not to assume things. One day after my mom yelled at me for ruining her birthday with another of Ariel's many 'stories', I told her to go away. Ariel didn't leave the day I went to the hospital for stitches, but she did leave many months later.

Why was my mom lying about that? Then my five-year-old words sprung back at me:

*"Daddy is sick. Ariel says if he doesn't see a doctor soon, he'll be as dead as a doornail."*

I always knew she didn't like the supernatural. I hadn't

realized it pertained to me until that specific moment.

"Where are you going?" I heard my mom's voice from behind me. I pivoted around and took a step back to stop her face from being right in mine.

If she talked about the ear clip one more time, I would snap. But yelling at Mom would get me grounded and I needed the freedom to ride my bike when being around her was...not to find a better word...explosive to my insides.

"I need some quiet for a report I have due tomorrow," I lied.

I needed to think and a house full of people wasn't the place and I needed that frigging ear clip. I'm sure with my luck it was on that boat still somewhere and that would lead right to me breaking the law again. I was thankful no one found it yet.

"Really Delia, you should have completed that before the party. Oh and I'm calling the company tomorrow to have your clip turned on remotely. We can find out where you lost it and retrieve it." She huffed at me.

*Shut up, Mom!* I thought, but something worse came out of my mouth.

"Mom, I cleaned, cooked and decorated for this party that I'm forced by obligation to attend. It's six p.m. I would like to do something for me, okay?" Mom's mouth dropped open and I turned away fearing the response.

"I'm going to someplace quiet." And I finished off my future freedom. I yelled the word "quiet"...that would equal grounding for embarrassing her.

Leaving before she could find a reason to stop me, I grabbed my bike and rode out of there. It took me twenty minutes to get up the courage. I had to turn onto the last beach on the street. It was a small memorial park with a wooden sign that read 'To my beloved, James Cross'. At my right was a big blue house with no fence separating the yard from the park. I always avoided this place before because it felt like I was trespassing in someone's backyard, but I needed that clip.

I left my bike without locking it to descend down those crumbling cement steps again and stopped at the open landing to make sure the boat was there. The sandy unkempt beach was riddled with sticks and trash, while cement rocks behind me had graffiti proclaiming love. I took it all in quickly, making sure no one was down there by the boat. The waves crashed from Lake Erie and echoed amongst the bluffs behind me. I wanted to make sure no one was on the beach.

"Hello," I yelled, out at the water, but the sound wouldn't carry past my face.

"Hello," a deep male voice said on my left. " Are you looking for something?"

I flung myself around and lost my balance and fell backward from the landing. He caught the front of my jacket, pulling me upward. I helped, climbing with my legs. He let go of my jacket when I was safely back on the landing.

Vulnerable on my side, I looked up from the ground at his figure above me so much my heart beat crazy with fear.

*'He is trying to help you,' I told myself, 'You are the one who just spazzed-out at him.'*

"Sorry. I didn't mean to scare you." He reached his hand out to help me up.

"Huh?" I couldn't think. Everything was hazy. Where was I? Maybe I did hit my head after all. I tried to make out his features to figure out his age.

"You really shouldn't be here by yourself. Sometimes we get drunks down here."

I sat up and decided to take his hand. He was maybe a year older than me and it seemed safe. As I was noticing his trench coat's torn pockets, it happened.

The moment our hands touched, intense sadness shook my whole body. It was like a great explosion all over. It took me a second to realize the source. My heart felt like someone was tearing it out.

The pain was so unmanageable. My body started to convulse. I could only explain this as death. I was dying.

# CHAPTER 03

"Are you ok?" His hands were on the sides of my head, speaking directly into my face, trying to get my attention.

Unable to speak, I pushed his hands away. My lungs stung cutting my breath short. I took three steps away trying to get my bearings. His face swam before my eyes and I realize the pain was dulling. Of course he was cute and I'd made an ass of myself, as usual. I needed to find a way to calm myself.

"Fine." I grunted in a caveman voice and then looked up at my knight.

That was what his face looked like to me, one of those fairytale knights or princes. His face was long and his hair, blond with long curls. He was so pleasant to look at except for his clothes, which were faded and showing their age.

He obviously wasn't from our neighborhood and must have been a runaway. Though, he was clean-shaven and I didn't detect a hint of B.O.

His green eyes carried something in them I recognized. Not tiredness or worry.

Who was in those eyes? I wondered.

"Is there anything I can do for you?" asked Derelict Prince.

It took me a moment to focus my breathing. If he was a prince I could at least speak like a lady. Right? Fat chance.

"Um, yeah, do you happen to know who owns that boat?" I asked, hoping he wasn't around.

"Yes. She lives in the blue house. Up there." He pointed. My head began to pound and I put my hand to my head rubbing two fingers between my eyebrows. I swayed and he caught my elbow.

"You should sit down."

"No, I just need to get something to drink." I stuttered.

My heart sped up and my body told me to run. I needed to end this conversation before I did anything else too conspicuous. He knew the owner after all. And besides that, he was too beautiful, the type that I would do anything for. I needed to get away. I controlled my world.

"I'll grab a bottle of water on the way home. Thanks for your concern." I started climbing the steps and my foot slipped, twisting my ankle.

'Crap,' I thought.

I felt his hand touch mine and the pain hit my heart again. The yelling started in my head this time because I didn't want another scene. I clamped my mouth shut trying not to scream, although it eventually became too much. I knew then that the pain was not from my ankle. I realized it was him. I was reacting to something in his touch.

"That's it." He picked me up and carried me up the steps.

"Hey," I responded, but I couldn't protest much. Talking was very difficult.

Before I knew it, we were at the top of the old steps. He carried me past the sign on the property that read 'No Trespassing' and sat me in the lounge chair on the patio.

"Are you crazy?" I started to say, but he was already entering the sliding glass door.

I sat there counting the seconds until the house alarm would sound and the police would charge me as an accessory to burglary. He came out before I could count to nine with an ice pack.

Wow! He was a resourceful beggar. Then it hit me. 'The

bum lives here, you idiot!'

"Is it swelling?" he asked. Then I studied his blond hair, the unusual bright kind that no one has unless they dyed it. His was like sunlight, not like bleach. He went to touch me again and I jumped up.

Shit, shit, shit, it's him. Gray sweatshirt!

I couldn't let the pain come back. I couldn't let him touch me. It was just too much... What was it? I think it was emotion, grief to be specific. Kind of like the intense sadness I felt when my dad died.

"Who died?" I asked, insensitive to his grief, as I put my hand over my heart trying to protect it.

"Did you know Lily?" His eyes looked right into mine and I saw it there. The gut wrenching pain I felt vibrated off him as I stood just in front of him.

"Wait a sec, you're the one that stole our boat the day of the attack. I have your ear clip by the way." He pointed an index finger. "Your hair was a different color and pulled back that day, right?"

My ankle was fine and I steadied myself. I felt embarrassment rising up in me and explode on my face in deep shades of crimson. I quickly turned, ran to my bike and peddled away as fast as possible. I knew I wasn't good with guys, but now I felt like a complete freak of nature. The klutzy thief tactic was not a way to meet guys. I knew how this was to play out; he had something on me and could use it to blackmail me. Why else had he not turned me in? The clip had my name in it.

I'd rather go to jail than end up a stranger's sex slave. Him being sexy to the point of confusion was beside the point. The guys at my school were a bunch of players. I was prepared for anything.

I peddled so hard I didn't see the truck pull into the driveway ahead of me. The Derelict bounded around the back of a red vapor waving his hands wildly. Fancy ride! Who was this jerk!

'Great. He was following me, perfect. No problem, I'd ride around him.' I thought.

"Wait. Please stop. You have to tell me your name," he pleaded and I stopped.

"Don't pretend you didn't look at my clip. Look, I can see you're having a hard time, but I really don't know you," I said horrified at my actions.

'Why did I stop my bike? You stole his boat you idiot. Run!' My thoughts screamed.

"For one, I didn't look at it; that's personal. And two, how do you know that about me?" He asked not angry or curious, but almost like he wanted me to think about it.

"I don't know. I can sort of feel it coming off you."

"You're an Empath then," he said softly, looking away as if talking to himself.

"No, I'm not…a what?" I stood there impatient and completely confused.

"An Empath," he said turning his attention back to me, "is someone who feels others' emotions. You felt something from me on the beach, didn't you?"

"I guess so. I don't know." I said crossing my arms.

"Please. Can I take you home? I really need to talk with you." He looked worried.

'What the hell was he worried about? I'm the one who should be worried. He has all the cards.' I wondered.

I was torn. I wanted to give him what he wanted, but my common sense told me to yell rape. I was afraid; the only thing a beautiful guy would want from me was a quickie. He had the leverage, too. He knew I was a thief.

"Hey you two, get the hell out of my driveway!" A short bald man yelled while he shook his fist at us from the front door of his house.

"Sorry, man. We're leaving." He spoke loudly but with a polite tone then turned his attention back to me. "Please say yes?"

I swear I saw his eyes got greener with his words and I felt a slight haze fill my head. I shook them off trying to focus. Why was it so hard to concentrate around him? I refused to be *that* girl who says yes to whatever a guy wants, even if he was delectable.

"Listen here. I'm not getting into a car with a perfect stranger." I stood my ground.

"Well you know my motorboat and where I live. We aren't complete strangers." He snickered and I fought the urge to punch him in the gut.

"What is your deal? Why haven't you called the police now or that night?"

"You're hurt and tired. Let me at least feed you. How about the diner around the corner?" He smiled so sweetly.

Damn. If I was going to say yes, it was going to be on my own terms.

"Fine. If you promise not to follow me home, I'll meet you there. I'm not getting into that thing with you." He could take me across the continent in four hours, no problem. Excellent for kidnapping anyone.

I pointed my finger, trying to look like I meant business Which I didn't, I looked ridiculous and overemotional as always.

"Deal," he said looking relieved.

At Claudia's Pancake Emporium I found him sitting in a booth by the window. His hair glistened annoyingly in the setting sun. Oh God, this was so stupid. I was going to sit across from him? Like a date?

The waitress was instantly there asking what we wanted.

"A piece of blueberry pie and coffee please," I said. I was so hungry I was shaking.

"Just coffee, please." His stare was intense which made me more nervous.

"Wow, a girl who eats sweets," he stated. The waitress poured the coffee into the cups already on the table.

"Yeah, well, life is to be lived. So does my stalker have

a name?" I asked as I looked out the window, still weary.

"Gregory James Carlisle. I was born here in Cleveland Gold Coast District on October 20th 2015."

Wow, was that more information than I needed. He was acting like I was going to do a background check. I wasn't planning on knowing him long enough to hire him. What job was he applying for anyway?

"You can call me Dee."

"Just Dee, huh?" He sounded disappointed that I didn't instantly trust him with my last name.

"Just because you gave me your name and birth date doesn't mean I'm going to tell you my life story." Why was he looking so scared?

"Okay, fine. I will also be turning seventeen in December," I grumbled hoping that would satisfy him for the moment.

"Tell me, Dee, does this hurt?" With his index finger he lightly drew a line from my left cheek to the bottom of my jaw, lifting my chin up slightly. A shiver went up my spine. This playful gesture caused a very different reaction than last time, one I didn't like at all. I took the irritation with myself and grew it in the Petri dish of my heart. I steadied my face showing no reaction.

"Sorry, I don't feel a thing," I said flatly.

There was something about him that made me want to tell him everything about myself, but that wasn't going to happen. I couldn't let him know there was a part of me that wanted more talking, and definitely more touching.

"Hmmm." He responded like he got his answer.

"What?" Please don't see through me.

"Don't you know?" He asked with an eyebrow arched.

"Can I have my ear clip back?"

"After." He brushed me off. "An Empathic ability is one of the hardest to handle."

"Oh yes, my ability," I rolled my eyes.

"Since the dome went up, there are lots of unusual things popping up. How long have you been able to feel what others feel?" He ignored my obvious mocking.

"Um, I don't know, always. Listen, are you going to turn me in or what? Why am I here with you?" I said out loud, but I was really asking myself.

"You are here because I wanted to talk with you about this."

The waitress brought the pie and laid the check on the table. I took a huge mouth full and made sure not to chew, sucking on it through my teeth.

"How do you know about the Empath thing?" I said and waved my fork as I talked and then I grinned with a mouth full of blueberries in my teeth. I wanted to seem unattractive; maybe he'd run away at my poor table manners.

"My grandmother is heavily into mysticism." He smiled slightly.

"My mom's Great Aunt Helen was like that too." I said, remembering her again. I was missing a piece of me and she had the answer. Her being dead wasn't going to stop me. I was determined to find out the truth.

"Really, you know where I'm coming from then."

"Yes, Gregory, I get the concept, but why am I having a date with a total stranger? Is this your thing? You leave boats unattended to blackmail girls into having pie with you?"

He didn't care about my rudeness and wanted to keep talking. How was I going to bail out of this one?

"So this is a date then?" He raised his right eyebrow again. It was irritating me the way he kept acting like he was figuring me out.

"Did someone die in your family? I mean, was I right?" I changed the subject to the first thing that came to mind.

It was harsh, but the question was eating at me. Also his 'on a date' question annoyed me, because I feared I would more than likely do anything for those green eyes. Getting pregnant before high school graduation wasn't in my top five.

I instantly regretted my coldness. I had hurt him again. He wasn't touching me, but his expression said it all. This was getting too close for me.

"Hey it's okay. I have to go anyway." I put my hands on the table to get up.

"No, no, please don't. My sister Lily she died in an accident about two months ago. When I caught you, the pain released a little and when I touched your face it went completely away. I don't know why I practically forced you here with me. I won't tell anyone about the boat. I don't care about that. All I can say is that it feels better to just be near you. You emanate peace," Gregory said, handing over my ear clip.

"Wow!" I said out loud looking down at my ear clip on the table.

As I placed it on my ear I thought, 'I emanate peace. What a complement! Crap! Hello teenage pregnancy! Don't look at him! He will know.'

He was unwrapping all the layers of protection that I acquired since my dad died so many years ago.

'Run! You must run now,' I told myself although he had just confided something very personal. I didn't want to hurt his feelings, but I needed those blankets around me to get through the day. This was my "mom shield" he was dissolving, and until I left for college, I would need it at full strength.

I told myself, 'Seem interested and then say you have to get home for curfew. After that, I'll get the hell out of here.'

"I mean wow that really sucks," I stammered while looking away. "I'm so sorry that happened to your family." I sounded robotic.

"Are you really?" His eyes squinted, almost trying to read my thoughts.

"Am I really what?" I asked innocently.

"Sorry. Your words are as unfeeling as your body language."

"I can't help that you don't like my sincerity," I hissed.

'He knows, run now!' I said to myself.

"You know my mom is expecting me for curfew. I must go!"

"Run, rabbit, run," he said sadly.

"Excuse me?" He caught me off guard with the strange phrase.

"Just something my mom used to say when I was found out. I would hide when I was caught in a lie."

"Well, you were lying when you said you don't know why you forced me here."

"Ah Empaths, you caught that…such great lie detectors."

"Goodbye, Gregory!"

I pressed my thumb to the check and the comp-table glowed. To my relief my clip acknowledged the payment. I feared it was damaged. Then I went through the door.

He was right there following behind me saying, "Meet me at the beach tomorrow at four?"

"Why would I do that?" I pointed my chin up. Standing right in front of him I realized how tall he was. His arms reached out to hold me there, but then reconsidered.

"Because I know what is happening to you and now that we have met, today is just the beginning."

Okay, this was getting creepy.

"Whatever, Gregory!" I turned and got on my bike. "If you follow me home, I will call the police. I don't care if you tell them the truth about the boat anymore." I rambled the threat.

That would do it. I wasn't afraid he'd hurt me, but if he thought I was, maybe he would leave me alone.

"It will only get worse. You know where I live, Dee. Anytime." I heard him call after me, but I wasn't looking back.

I was afraid if I did, his eyes would hypnotize me and I would never be able to go. I wanted to be near him always and that scared me worse than anything.

# CHAPTER 04

Too many different vehicles filled my driveway and flowed all the way down the street in a stream. Most were segues, there was a couple old groundhogs. Only the most nostalgic drove those four wheeled contraptions. But not one Vapor. Vapors are reserved in my mind for pricks now. To my irritation, my mother's party probably wouldn't end until ten and it was only eight. I wanted to be alone in my room without someone poking their head in with some annoying party-pooper comment.

"No thank you, Uncle Sean." I called as I bounded in the door and up the stairs. "I don't want to play corn-hole right now!"

A buzzing started to reverberate in my head. Two of my Uncles were yelling about the attacks and the buzz got louder as they did.

"What do you mean we should release the protection field as a sign of good faith?" one said.

"Showing vulnerability is the only way to bring peace," Uncle Sean declared.

Closing my door with my head underneath my pillow to block the rest out, I hummed Twinkle, Twinkle Little Star. My whole head was on fire and just when I couldn't take it any longer, I ran to the bathroom and threw up. As people left my mother's party, so did the buzzing, and then came sweet silence. I remembered what Gregory said and I groaned at the notion that he could be right.

The next morning I awoke to my mother's shrill voice sounding from the bathroom door.

"Delia, why are you asleep on the bathroom floor? Are you sick?"

"You didn't get into the beer last night did you?" she asked, shoving open the door, forcing me to get away from behind it.

Good old mom always looked for the best in me. If she knew me at all she'd know I didn't even like the way drinking made me feel. She loved to jump all over me even if I was sick.

"You should stay home. I don't want to be accused of giving a minor alcohol," Mom said, with her hands on her hips.

"N-no, I'm fine Mom." I stammered pushing past her in the doorway.

I had to go to school or I wouldn't be allowed to go to the beach at four. I needed to see Gregory one more time for research purposes only, of course. I was still mad that he could see through my bull but I just wouldn't let him get to me. I couldn't. I needed my security blanket of manipulation, otherwise I would have to let him in to see the real me. And I didn't know if I liked me.

"Probably why you were so mouthy with me last night. That earned you extra chores after school by the way." She stopped me.

No! I have to see him. I thought.

"I can't. I have a project I'm working on with a partner," I lied and then ran for my bedroom.

She didn't follow behind but I heard her say, "I want you home by six."

School was a buzz of people and I did my best not to get sick. I took a history test which I was sure I failed. The buzz always got more intense when people fought or were sad. I stopped going to my locker because the girl next to me just broke up with her boyfriend. It was when she slapped him that the hum became a loud buzz again.

"What the hell are you looking at? You want to get slapped, too?" Winter Swanson snarled at me as I stared. Her fury pulsed through me and I wanted punch something.

"Nope." I gritted through my teeth, holding back.

All those emotions you experience in a troubled relationship pumped through my head. He was jealous, she felt trapped, and with the both sides of the argument whirling around me, I was forced to run to the toilet. Lunch was not on the agenda so I spent it in the library, researching the word Empath. There was some information about a Sumerian god named Enki and how his empathic ability saved humanity from his evil brother Enlil. But nothing that told me how to keep dinner down. After school, I prepared myself to see Gregory Carlisle one more time.

I biked to that small memorial beach while my heart swelled with fear and excitement. 'Please be there,' I thought. I needed to see him, to be near him, even if it hurt. I peddled as fast as I could from my school to the beach. Relief passed over me when I saw him standing at the steps. He shook his head smiling.

"I thought you were mad at me. So what happened? Did you throw up yet?"

"Yes, twice," I grimaced. I proceeded to tell him about my day, which he found quite interesting.

"You have to learn how to let it flow over you. You can't control what people throw at you, so fighting is not an option. If you fight it, it will inevitably knock you on your butt every time."

"How did you know it was me after I brought the boat back?"

His shoulders tensed up for a minute. "It was the blood you left on the boat. Normal people don't bleed like that unless they're dying of a fatal wound. I found your ear clip when I was cleaning it up."

"Oh I forgot about that. I can't remember a lot about that day. I'm sorry about the mess."

"No problem," he shrugged.

We sat there for a while in silence except for the constant waves whooshing. I relaxed. It was nice, a little too nice. I wanted to put my head on his shoulder.

Delia Stanton doesn't lean on anybody, I reminded myself.

Getting up, I had made my decision not to come back. He grabbed the arm of my coat causing me to jump out of my thought process.

"You will come back," he said.

It was a strange statement, more of a command. I looked at him with my mind spinning. He wanted me around. I found that strangely comforting. Usually I pushed people away because I freaked them out by the things I'd say. Just like the day I met Gregory, I didn't mean to talk about his pain. As the pain a person experienced erupted, inside me I would blurt out how they felt before they could process it themselves. Now, I saw why some might find it irritating or even scary.

"Sure," I shrugged.

"Tomorrow at four?" He smiled.

I didn't answer. I was getting this confusing feeling of wanting to stay and wanting to run away. I chose the latter because it was what I was used to. It was safer for me to keep people at a distance, but I couldn't stop thinking about him.

When I got home, I lay in my bed listening to mine and my dad's favorite band, Tag that Kid, thinking about Gregory, the delectable derelict from the beach.

That night my dreams were a mixture of memories of Great Aunt Helen and of monsters made of ten-foot shadows. In them I was three again and we were playing my game of nurse where she allowed me to shove the pills forcefully into her mouth while she laughed heartily. Then she drew me close so my mom couldn't hear. "I'm going to be leaving you soon, my Sunshine. Everyone will be saying I'm gone, but I will only be asleep. You are not to get upset about anything pertaining to me leaving because I'll come back to you later. I'll look different and we won't be able to play the same ways we always do, but I'll be watching over you. Do you know that we have a lot in common? We are a lot alike."

"No, we are not. You are big and I'm little," I said pretentiously.

She laughed again in her patient way. "No, we have the same way of feeling things the way my grandmother did. I often feared this ability,as it was not accepted in my time during the 1920's and 30's. So I pushed it away, but you must embrace this thinking. Do not be afraid. This life means nothing if you don't live it. You will see objects and people that others cannot. The veil will lift the more you will it. I love you, my Sunshine." Then she sang, "You are my Sunshine. My only Sunshine…"

And then I was at her wake, telling my mother not to cry, as Aunt Helen was just asleep, when I saw two men approach Aunt Helen's coffin. They both had large shadows that danced behind them even though there were no other shadows being made by the other friends and family members in the room. I left my mother, drawn to the two young men. As I got closer I could hear what they were saying.

"She has no children and thus no grandchildren. I think we are safe in assuming the family line has been exterminated." I heard one say to the other.

"There is still the house of Cross that can bring about the cleansing."

"No, they will need the leader and she is the only descendent, this Bracken. We are safe."

"I don't care. I'm still going to keep an eye on the Carlisle twins. Their abilities are starting to show already. The one called Lily is a major threat."

"Do as you wish, but we have nothing to worry about now from my former bride."

I was standing right next to them but they couldn't see me. I noticed a light flashing like a large fire fly coming from the inside of their coats. I had the worst urge to run up and catch it. There was something wrong about the light like I needed to fix it. But I was only three and was distracted soon by a stick of bubble gum my Uncle Sean waved in front of me.

I awoke the next morning thinking of what Gregory said a couple days before. His sister's name was Lily, Gregory and Lily Carlisle. No, it was only a dream, not a memory, I told myself. I knew all that stuff because Gregory had told me.

After school everyday for a month, I would meet him at the small memorial beach. We would talk for five minutes then sit in silence until I got nervous and ran away.

Most days at school were not as hard but were still difficult. I tried to let the emotions flow through me but I found myself becoming personally attached. If someone laughed, I laughed. If someone was sad, I held onto that sadness.

I went up to my Physics teacher one day to ask for a pass to the infirmary because I was considering going home. I could tell he was tired. When he handed me the pass my stomach exploded with pain. Both of us grabbed our stomachs at the same time, but I was the one that threw up in his trashcan. I saw the antacids on his desk and I said as I left, "You really should go to a doctor. It's like you have ulcers or something." His eyes were as wide as saucers. Apparently I was right about something.

The nurse wanted to call my mom but I insisted that I was all right. I thought it over, and if I went home, I had no way of telling Gregory I wasn't coming. I didn't have his mobile code yet and I didn't want to just not show up. Truth be told, I wanted to see him more each day. The compulsion to see him was starting to override the scary need to run away.

He never tried to touch me since the first day. Sometimes I wanted him to but he seemed to know I was skittish. When I rode my bike that same day to see him, I thought about what would happen if I touched him again.

Would it hurt like the first time or feel really nice like the third? When I told him about throwing up at school again, he told me to hold out my hand.

He seemed hesitant when he asked, "Can I try something?" Then he held his hand lightly above mine.

"I guess so. Hey, they're your shoes!" I teased, but I really didn't want to embarrass myself again by getting sick on him.

"Now breathe slowly, in through your nose and out your mouth. Try to relax." I looked at Lake Erie, not his hand.

He lightly brushed my palm with his and I saw something in my mind. It was blurry, but it was something. He did it again and I saw a teenage girl laughing on a carousel. She was still, like a picture. Frozen for all time in his memory.

"Uh…" I sighed.

"Do you see something?

"Yes, a girl on a carousel." I said.

"That was Lily the day we went to Cedar Point. She loved anything that spins. I was thinking of that on purpose. It was my last happy memory I remember having before the accident."

"I know it felt happy, but… doesn't it make you sad too?"

"Normally it would, but you have this way of making it all okay. You make me feel differently about my memories of her." He touched my face the same way he did in the diner. I saw myself through his eyes and I knew he wanted to be more than just friends.

"Oh!" I couldn't say it but the little girl that read Sleeping Beauty over and over till the binding broke screamed, "Me, too!" His eyes were searching for something in mine.

"I know we haven't known each other very long, but I wanted you to know that I mean you no harm. You see, I care for you quite a bit already."

Oh…my…God! He could open me up and I hated that. I couldn't navigate this where I wanted it to go. My heart fluttered and my face rushed red. I turned my back so he couldn't see the embarrassment on my face.

He pushed his face into my hair. His lips nuzzled my ear. I was giving a little more inside with every breath.

"Tell me how you feel. Please...if there is one thing I don't want to do, it's scare you."

"I must seem so childish to you." I shook my head at my inability to figure this out.

"No, it is just normal Empath stuff. You had to be closed off because you didn't know what was happening to you. The lake helps you block out the noise. Doesn't it?"

"How do you know so much about being Empathic?"

"My sister was one and my grandma is Psychic." He smiled.

"My Great Aunt Helen was said to be Psychic...it must run in my family the gene then, like your family. I've been thinking about Great Aunt Helen a lot lately. She told me she would come to me after she died. I found out from my uncle that I had an imaginary friend, and it must have been her."

"This Great Aunt Helen, her last name wasn't Bracken, was it?" He took my hand in his.

"No, her last name was Chase." The demons in my dream called her Bracken.

"Huh!" His eyes were wide with astonishment, looking at our hands linked.

"What?" I was deep in thought.

"Nothing." He dismissed. "Hey, it doesn't hurt you to be near me now. I guess because I don't hurt anymore when I'm around you. It's like you absorb pain."

"Great, like I don't have enough problems. Now I get everyone else's pain too."

My mobile clip sounded. "Oh it's Mom." I rolled my eyes.

"Aren't you going to answer that?"

"No, then she'll see I'm not where I'm supposed to be and I'll have to explain where I am."

"Then go ahead."

"My mom will break the dome if she thinks I'm at the beach by myself. I froze the tracker to show I'm at the school still."

"So tell her you're with me." His hands gestured, "Hello, I'm here."

"She hasn't met you yet. How do I explain meeting you? I stole your boat, Gregory. We don't even go to the same school and we live in separate cities."

"Dee, I want you to be very honest with your mom from now on, especially when it pertains to me."

"Why?" I was amazed he cared, but he was getting involved in something that was none of his business.

"Because lies are self-made jail cells. I don't want barriers keeping you from me. If your mom finds out you're secretly seeing some guy, and you know she will eventually, then she will be suspicious of me. I want her to trust me which means she has to trust you first." His eyes turned greener.

I was getting a strange pull to do whatever he said. Why was he getting irritated? Why did he care? I was pretty sure despite my lack of experience that most guys didn't think twice about sneaking around.

"Please, Dee. You have been hiding yourself away from her probably because you feel her emotions more deeply then anyone else. If she's hurting, so are you, and if you're both hurting, that can seem insurmountable to live with. Has there been any reason for her to be in tremendous pain?"

"You won't understand." I felt the tears rise up. I never cried. What the hell!

"Tell me," he whispered. I got dizzy as I always did around him. Stupid hormones took over whenever I was near him.

"I predicted my dad's death and for that she'll never forgive me."

"What do you mean you predicted his death?"

He sounded upset with me.

"I-I…" I tried to get it out but it sounded crazy.

He turned my body around facing him and said, "I need you to tell me exactly how you knew he was going to die." His words echoed inside side my head looking for their home, the truth.

"I had an imaginary friend when I was five or six and she told me Dad needed to go to the doctor or he'd die. And when the cancer ate him up, he died five years later. After that, I couldn't breathe when I was around my Mom. It was like all the oxygen was sucked out of the room. I pushed her away and we stopped talking. I thought we were growing apart. I never remembered the prediction until the day I met you, but now I know for sure it was the reason." What the hell! I didn't want to say any of that.

Gregory grabbed a hold of me when he felt me sway. Then it came. I gulped at the pain in my throat, forcing tears back, but it was too late, the hot wetness was all over my face. There was that hole again but it was not from him. This time it was my own grief.

"You never cried for your dad, did you?" he whispered. "Wouldn't it be a good idea to talk to your mom right now?"

'No! No! No!' My head screamed but my heart spoke, "Please take me home. I need to talk to her."

He nudged me forward to his truck. I had to show him the way to my house, which was really hard when tears kept welling up faster than I could wipe them away. I ran out of the car before Gregory could put it in park. I stomped up the porch and the screen door banged at my hastiness.

"Mom," I yelled down the main hallway. "Mom, I'm so sorry." I found her in the kitchen and immediately hugged her possibly the first time since before my dad passed. Was this a dream?

"What? What is this? And who are you?" Her eyes stared at Gregory standing in the doorway.

"I'm sorry I upset you and said those horrible things to

you about Dad dying."

There it was, the pain of a grieving widow. The ache of losing a companion you've talked, laughed, and laid with every night, because they were your true happiness. It came out of her the same way it did with Gregory and dumped itself right on top of my pain. I had the worst urge to slap her away like you might a searing hot poker. But instead I accepted it and then let it go.

"We don't talk about that." My mother stiffened.

"But you will because she needs you to," Gregory interrupted.

"You think I killed him," I sobbed.

"You'll tell Delia she didn't, right?" Gregory said tipping his slightly as if to listen to a secret. "You will comfort her."

"You have done nothing you should feel guilty about." Her eyes watched him closely. "Not that I mind, but what brought this on?" She looked him up and down once again.

"Um…I was just talking and this kind of came up." I blew my nose and wiped my eyes.

"Yes, but honey, who is your friend?" She was anxious to get information.

"His name is Gregory. We met at the memorial beach about a month ago when we had that party."

"You lied to me? Why?" The anger in her voice bubbled.

"Let her finish." He said. "Go on, Delia."

"I wanted to get out of the house. I was suffocating with all those people here. Mom, I needed to leave and ride my bike and I knew you would want a reason. So I gave you one. Gregory lives right next to the beach there. He saw me go down there alone and worried about me. I went there again today because I wanted to see him. We were talking and this came up. When I needed to talk to you, he brought me home."

'Are you crazy?' I asked myself. 'She will never let you leave the house again. And you haven't even said a word about stealing his boat.' But it uncontrollably flowed from me like an open wound.

My mom looked shocked. She paused for about a minute. I think that was the most I had said to her in years. I never explained my feelings to her. I shivered waiting for her to blow.

"You will forgive her with all she's been through today." Gregory smirked an odd smile.

"It will be alright, Delia." She patted my arm. "Is there anything I can get you Gregory, something to drink maybe?"

"Oh, no thank you." He stood there not fazed in the slightest.

"Call me Sheila. Are you sure?"

"Yes, Sheila. Thank you anyways," he said, looking down.

After promising my mom I'd never lie to her again, she in turn promised to give me all the space I needed. She trusted me for the first time to make my own decisions. She did a complete one eighty in less than ten minutes. I was sure her reaction was going to be rash, but Gregory was right. Telling her worked. It was like he was guiding me to a better existence by teaching me how to live with this affliction.

When I woke up the next morning it was to the sound of my mom laughing. I got ready and went to get breakfast. As I entered the kitchen I was startled to find Gregory there, eating.

"What are you doing?" I sniped.

"Eating. Good morning Delia." He had a fork full of eggs in his mouth.

"Okay, I can see that, but what are you doing here?"

He had caught me off guard and I didn't like it. Just because he drove me home yesterday didn't mean he could waltz in here anytime he wanted.

"Your mom asked me last night when I was leaving to come for breakfast."

"Well I have school in an hour." I needed some space to

think and he knew too much about me.

"You're not going today, honey." My mom interjected with a Step-ford smile.

"Huh? Today is Tuesday isn't it?" I glared at Gregory.

"Well I was thinking that you needed to take a mental health day. You dealt with a lot yesterday, Delia. A day of fun will do you some good. So you and Gregory are going to play hooky." She said.

"Don't you go to school?" I was pointing my finger at him like an accusing child.

"Nope. I have a tutor. I'm home-schooled." His smile irritated me.

He never told me that! I guess I never asked him. Come to think of it we barely talked the past month. Well, I was going to take an interest from here on out. This was obviously his idea and my mom hadn't a clue. Poor thing probably thought she came up with it on her own. I was jealous of his power over her. Then I realized he had the same power over me and I was annoyed that he could control the situation so easily.

"Of course you are." I snapped. "But Mom-"

"No, it's too late." She cut off my whining. "I already called the school. You two have fun. I'm already late for work." She pushed Gregory and me out and closed the door in my surprised face. I stood there with my nose pressing against it, stunned.

"What the…"

"Come on, let's go get you some breakfast." Gregory put his arm round me.

"You already ate, remember?" I glared up at him.

He tipped his head back and was smiling up to the sky. "Ah Delia, you are so gullible."

I was getting in his Vapor, but I was angry. "Why are you calling me Delia?" I crossed my arms over the worn seatbelt. I couldn't let him in again. Things were moving too fast.

"You never told me what Dee stood for and when

I heard your mom called you Delia, I decided I liked it better."

"You decided. Aren't you on your high horse, assuming what you can decide for me today?"

"Don't you want to spend time with me?" His big green eyes were so innocent they made my icy exterior melted instantly. Crap, what was he doing to me? I was pathetic.

"Where are we going anyways?" I said through gritted teeth.

"I want you to meet my Grandmother."

"So we are going…?"

"My house, you know the one next to the beach where we first met." The sarcasm made me want to hit him but curiosity stopped me. New possibilities flooded my mind. I could get a glimpse of his room and get some dirt on him, too.

"I have never been in a house on the lake before. What is it like waking up to breathtaking sunrises every morning?"

"I don't know. I never get up that early. I guess you sort of take it for granted when you grow up with it."

"You have to promise me you'll get up and see it tomorrow morning."

"Nope. Only if you're there with me." My heart jumped. It was so unfair how he could affect me in that way.

As we pulled in the driveway, I saw how big the house was at that angle. It seemed so natural being there at his house, like I belonged there.

'It must be the lake's soothing effect,' I told myself but it was more than that. I was meant to be there. I was home.

We went through the garage door to a very impressive kitchen. Gregory's grandmother was at the stove cooking eggs and pancakes. The table was set with a huge stack in the middle though there wasn't any butter or syrup in sight.

"You're right on time as always, Greggy."

"Hi Grandma. This is Delia. She's going to join us for breakfast."

"Hi Delia. I'm Nola. It is nice to meet you. Now go on and eat, you two, before it gets cold." She ushered us toward the table with her palms open and a big smile.

I was very comfortable as if she was my grandma and he was the guest. As I ate the first bite, I realized I didn't need to put anything on them. This was weird. I never ate my pancakes plain. I was afraid 'Greggy' might laugh at me but he appeared to be doing the same exact thing.

"Wow, these are amazing." I covered my mouth, still chewing.

"After years of practice with herbs and spices, you learn a thing or two. My secret with pancakes is simple. Just add an extra yolk, lots of cinnamon and use wholegrain flour. Oh, and lots of love, of course." She pinched Greggy's right cheek and I wickedly smiled at him. She was sweet, but she was giving me plenty of ammunition to tease him with later. Thank you, Nola!

I studied her face and there were only laugh lines around her eyes and mouth. She had absolutely no sunspots at all which amazed me because my mother had some developing already. Her apron covered a floral dress that made a swishing sound as she walked.

"How are you adjusting to being an Empath, Delia?" She asked this question like I had just gotten my ears pierced.

She was excited for me, obviously, though I didn't share her enthusiasm. My ears stopped hurting after a day and the pain of everybody in my head has been a life sentence.

"Not well."

"I could teach you ways of controlling those sensations, if you wanted me to. I taught Greggy's sister when she was your age. Rest her soul." Her eyes saddened and my heart tingled slightly.

"Yes, of course. I would love any help you could give me. It is not like they teach intro courses on this somewhere. Do they?" I glanced at Greggy, who was smiling.

"No, unfortunately they don't. It is too bad for those who are born with a gift and never fully get to use it. Most of the time people deny what is happening. It is very sad." He was so earnest when he said this I knew that he was serious.

"I had no idea what *this* was until I met you, Gregory, and then everything made sense. I would probably still not know if it weren't for you." Nola dropped her fork onto her plate making a clanging noise.

"You didn't tell her?" She looked at him incredulously.

"No. She has been so closed off by her dad's death that I haven't had the chance." He whispered like I wasn't there.

"Tell me what?" How dare he bring that up right now? I was enjoying myself.

"Honey, we have been expecting you. We have been leaving the keys in the ignition of that motorboat for more than a year. I am Psychic just as you are an Empath. I have seen you in my dreams many times. You are destined to do great things with the right guidance and love." She nodded toward Gregory on the word love. Nola looked scared like I might bolt with this new information.

I knew she was telling the truth because my heart confirmed it. The truth was undeniable. The prediction of my dad's death and my Great Aunt Helen both popped into my head again. Things were coming together. I was trying to slow down my thoughts but more kept coming.

'Delia you have to relax' I told myself, 'you don't want to…'

"There you are! You have been passed out for almost ten minutes." Gregory was standing over me as I lay on a big green sofa. "Grandma said it was a not good idea to have you sniff smelling salts because your mind needed time to work things out on its own."

"Thanks." I took a glass of water from Nola and sat up slowly. I was in shock, unable to absorb the reality yet.

Gregory took my hand to help me up. My heart then told me that Gregory was afraid. "What is going on behind those eye?" He was almost begging.

"I don't know but your fear is not helping me. I won't jump up and leave, I promise. So calm down, Greggy." I got him to smile. His smile warmed me up and I was able to stand. "Can I go outside and sit on your patio for awhile? I need a minute to think."

"Of course, dear," said Nola.

As I sat there on a wooden swing, the anger slowly twisting into me. There it was, a sense of purpose I didn't want. I wished this wasn't happening to me. I wanted to live for me and no one else!

"Why me?" I said out loud feeling my face becoming wet. *Crying again, great,* I touched my face. *I'm weaker than I thought. How was a person like me going to solve the problems of the world?*

The lake was too quiet and calm. I wanted waves high and crashing to mimic my frustration. I decided to yell the universe for this. "You couldn't have me levitate or control weather? No, I get to feel all the crap in the world. Oh, and here is the cherry on top of my crap sundae: I have a great purpose as if I didn't have enough pressure figuring what to do with my life."

"You're not a super hero or a normal person. You are an Empath. There are plenty of great people in history who had the same pressures put on them. You are special, so deal with it. I wish someone would give me a heads up on my part in this world. I envied my sister and I envy you. I wish I had a purpose already set for me."

"How am I supposed to do these great things when I don't even know what my favorite color is? I have no hobbies. I don't have any good friends that I hang out with anymore. I have no idea who I am. Someone made a big mistake up there, Gregory! I will fail the world and I will definitely fail you, so you should walk away now while you can because I'm not worth it."

"You shut up!" He screamed with tears in his eyes. His hands held my shoulders, slightly shaking me. "I have been waiting for you for more than a year. I won't have you talk about yourself like that. You're worth it, or you wouldn't be here. So listen up to your first official purpose: letting me love you."

He grabbed me so tight that I couldn't continue my tantrum. I felt at first a need from him but I didn't understand. Then he pulled my body to his and kissed me hard. Though I knew he was trying to kiss the sense into me, I didn't care about anything but his consciousness inside me. He loved me. I knew that now and it made me open up to the many challenges that awaited me. There was a feeling of static electricity in the air and I knew that everything was as it should be. I was sure about one thing: Gregory had an ability, and it was well developed. He could convince me of anything.

"Let me help you find out who you are?" He whispered softly in my ear. My legs were numb and he was holding me up in his arms so they wouldn't give out.

"Okay," was all I could choke out.

As he walked me back to his Vapor, I came to the conclusion that I was falling in love with him, too, and I barely knew a thing about him. I wondered where his parents were.

"Why do you live with Nola and not your parents?" I asked.

He shrugged, "My mom was diagnosed with schizophrenia when I was five and my dad couldn't handle it and left. Then my grandma moved us here and tried to take care of my mom the best she could, but she was forced to put her in an institution a year later."

"Oh, I'm so sorry." I put my hands up, surrendering, still embarrassed of my bad behavior the day we met. "Really, I mean it this time."

"I know when you're being sincere. You get these big cow eyes." He opened his eyes really wide and fluttered them.

I hadn't laughed so hard in a really long time. I was happy for the first time in three years and it was entirely his fault.

# CHAPTER 05

I went back to school the next day, even though I'm sure Gregory could have talked my mom into a whole week if he wanted to. He had this way about him that made me pissed off and adore him at the same time. He took me on a tour of what I would come to know as the Cross House, which was named after his Great Grandfather who built the house for his bride in 1926. He showed me an aged black and white picture with two well-dressed people that stood in front of a newly built version of the house.

"That's the day they moved in. Come on. I have to show you my favorite place in the whole wide world." He grabbed my hand.

He took me into an elevator (Yes, an elevator!) that was really cool but really old and scary. We went past the second floor up to what must have been a third floor. When the doors opened the gates of the old elevator, I stood there in awe, unable to move.

"Are you okay?" He smiled pulling me into a very large ballroom that was completely encased in glass.

Even though it was a very gray fall day, it was like being on top of the world. To the right was the city miles away, and though I knew that there were taller buildings there, you felt like you were looking down on Cleveland. You could see the protection fields glistening with the sun's rays. I had heard at certain angles they were possible to spot their prism effect of dancing rainbows. The drones scurried as usual like dogs trying to find bones.

"Our gilded cage…" I surmised softly.

"I'm sorry?"

"Have you ever wondered why the other countries hate us?"

"All I know is what I learned in school." He shrugged. "The US has a device that others both want and fear. I'm guessing the books mean the protection field?"

"But the others must have technology that is similar," I wondered. "Their drones are identical to ours. It's like they're not telling us something."

"Think about your ability. There are plenty of gifted children, but they're never publicized. Ever since the US Internet was cut from the world by the protection field radiation, we only hear what they want us to. I'm sure there are plenty of untold secrets we'll never know." Gregory shook his head.

"When I was little I did a report on Paris, France. I told my parents I wanted them to take me right there. That was the day I learned we weren't really free but caged zoo animals. My dad cried when he told me it wouldn't be possible then or maybe ever."

"You are meant to bring about change, Delia. Maybe one day we will go together." He hugged me. The word together made me shiver. The churning conversation started to make me nervous.

"Uh, this room is huge." I said pulling away and looking around for a change in subject.

"This was a ballroom once. Now it is our meditation room. There hasn't been a party in here since my parents wedding."

"Why not?"

"My Grandpa died a year later and Grandma just didn't have it in her to celebrate. She used to have regular parties for holidays, friends birthdays and such. I have seen pictures. They were spectacular. My mom told me once, at night when the stars can be seen with the lights of the city, it's like being in heaven. The night of the attack I saw for myself. She was right."

"You can't even see this room from the road." I was amazed.

"The house was built at a special angle to disguise this room so you couldn't see the kind parties that were being held."

"I don't understand."

"Well, you see…the house was built during prohibition."

"So your great grandparents were lawbreakers?" I teased.

"Even worse. They would have boats sent from Canada to the beach down below."

"Can you imagine? So they were bootleggers! How exciting!" I exclaimed.

"What else would you expect from two Nuevo Rich Irish-Americans? If Mohammad couldn't go to the mountain?"

"Yeah, yeah, yeah, I got it. The mountain came here. Right?"

"My great-grandfather moved many mountains to make my great-grandmother, Juniper, happy. She loved having her big lavish parties. Or so what Grandma has told me. Even during the Great Depression they would spare no expense."

"Wasn't that considered tacky?" I said with yet again no filter.

"Her parties became charity events mainly for the destitute and orphaned children. Although, she had a hard time getting the others who survived the crash to attend because by then she was considered to be what the rich called eccentric."

"Anyone who wants to help children can't be that wacky." I conceded.

"Well she was Psychic and didn't hide it. I think people feared her, even the ones whom she warned about the crash and basically saved their livelihood still turned their backs on her."

"How awful," I said.

"She had my Grandma by then to keep her busy. She also had people who worked for her she loved and trusted." He went over to the Lyra player and turned it on. He came back, put his hands on my waist and drew me close.

"What?" I had no clue what it was he wanted me to do.

"It's an ancient ritual people who are dating sometimes do. It's called dancing." He smiled.
"I haven't danced since…" His feet…my dad used to let me stand on his feet and we would dance together.

"Sshh…just listen to the lyrics. I chose this song especially for you." It wasn't a slow romantic song. It was peppy. The lyrics slightly echoed through the hall. "Let me un-shadow your heart."

"Nice. Who was it?"

"You don't know Prank the Mind?"

"Uh no…I um really not into music. Occasionally I'll listen to U2 or Tag that Kid on a CD my dad gave me."

"CD? You're kidding right?"

"Yeah, so what? I'm not into music."

"Let me see your clip." His hand started to go to my right ear and I pushed it away.

"No." I said ducking but he already unlatched the inserted ring from my ear and was applying it to his.

"Give it back." I went to grab it but he had his hand over his ear.

"Lyra- Library." He commanded laughing and I could see his eyes moving back and forth but I knew there was nothing to read.

"It's empty, not surprising." He shrugged.

"Whatever!"

"Listening to music is what teenagers do, Delia.

How are we supposed to generate and get through the angst and rebellion without it?" He took my hand and started out of the room. "We need to get you some hobbies and fast. Come on."

We took the stairs this time to the second floor and down to the end of the hallway he opened the door to the colors of the Cleveland Browns. The curtains were orange, the walls a deep brown and a white bedspread with an orange helmet embroidered on it.

"Is this your room?"

"Hell, no. I am strictly a Steelers fan. I swear she rooted for the Browns just to piss me off." She? Oh crap! This was Lily's room? He walked over to her bag and rummaged through it.

"What are you doing?" I asked in horror.

I felt really uncomfortable being there. It was like she still was alive living there, with her dirty clothes still in a basket near front of her bed. Even though I didn't know her, I was on edge, thinking at any moment she would come in yelling at us to get the hell out of her room.

"Here it is." He was trying to hand me something that belonged to her.

"Whoa," I put my hands up palms out and backed a step away. "No, thank you."

"It's okay, Delia. She would have really liked you and would have let you borrow it anyway. Especially once she found out how musically deficient you truly are. You have no idea how sad it would have made her. She loved all kinds of music from classical to quels."

"I don't know." I said as he took my opened hand and placed the indigo clip into it.

"It's her music clip."

"I know what a Lyra Clip looks like," I mumbled.

"Then why don't you have one? Don't you ever listen to even the radio in the car?"

"Why do you care?"

"Because it's weird, Delia. You've cut yourself off from the world completely since your dad died."

"That's not true."

"Oh yeah? Okay, I'll prove it to you. What's your favorite show?"

"I don't watch screen."

"Then what is it you like to do?"

"I don't know…I like to read sometimes." He immediately touched my clip on his ear.

"Logo- Library." He commanded. "There's nothing here, Delia, but school books."

"So?" God, what did he care!

"You like to go to book stores then?" He asked.

"No." I shrugged.

"So you go to the old libraries?"

"No."

"Then where do you get the books you read?"

"My room." I shrugged.

"And how many hand held books do you have, Delia?"

"I don't know...about seventy. They were my dad's except for a couple hand-me-down story books."

"So you have reread the same seventy books over and over again for the past three years."

"I guess so." I shrugged.

"I'm not trying to make you feel bad. I want to show you that you aren't growing. You have stopped everything, keeping the world as you know it, to include only that which you did with your dad and nothing else. He read you those books before you went to bed, didn't he?"

"No," I said at first but then fessed up. "I read them out loud to him. Even toward the end we kept our ritual. I like our rituals."

"What else is there?"

"Listen, I told you already about this. That I don't have any direction and-"

"There is a difference between not knowing who you are and just avoiding trying anything new all together. You think it's safer because you're afraid."

Safe was my word and afraid was not. He had a lot of nerve putting the two together. At the time in my mind, one did not pertain to the other at all.

"I. Am. Not. Afraid!" My voice was slightly yelling.

"Oh, yeah! I just proved that you are hiding. Now it's your turn to show me you're not afraid. Here is the charging pad for Lily's Lyra and Logo. Show me exactly how wrong I am!" I grabbed the two and walked out of Lily's room, down the stairs and out the door to Gregory's truck. Without a word, he drove me home, though I was so mad I could've walked the whole way.

Dear Gregory,

I am ignoring your calls for a reason. I have nothing to say right now and you'll just push me into talking about it some more. Call you in a few days, Delia

"She doesn't want to see you today, Gregory." I heard my mother say down the hall through my bedroom doorway.

"Please just tell her to come to the door. It's been four days. I have a quick question for her."

"That's funny. She was expecting you'd say that and told me to give you this when you did." I smiled and congratulated myself on being right. I had actually predicted that he would come today.

I imagined Mom handing him the note I wrote earlier as a look of irritation would spread across his face because he wasn't getting his way.

"You are wrong, you know." His voice came from behind me.

He was there standing next to me. I was so lost in thought, priding myself I didn't hear him enter my room.

Damn it. I guess I lost that one. I thought to myself.

"You're fired, Mom!" I yelled to her from my room.

"Sorry, but he can be very convincing." She called back lightly. Then I turned my attention to Gregory.

"Get out! Don't you get it? I don't want to see you." I said as I stood and pointed my finger at the door. I was so angry I couldn't see straight. How was he able to make things go his way all the time?

"Yeah, well, like I care what you want. Why aren't you answering my calls?" He said.

"I am tired of talking." I said and his body softened a little in its stance.

"So let's not talk, let's go do something. It's the last few days before Cedar Point closes for the winter. Let's go." At that moment when he said, "Let's go," my perception momentarily shifted from dark and narrow to bright and happy, but I held onto my dark place.

A few days ago Gregory made me look at the things that were painful, and I wanted none of that right now. I needed to push him away. I needed space from that pain.

"Why would I want to go on roller coasters with you, when this whole relationship has been one big ride?" I said and he locked his eyes onto mine. I felt my anger fading.

"If you go with me, it can be the start of us making our own memories together." He said it so sweetly that it drew me in.

"It can?" I was getting confused. I was mad at him, right? Yes. I was mad at him for…

"Yes. You don't want to waste such a nice Sunday indoors, do you?" He asked. He was so close to my face. I felt his breath against my cheeks.

"No, that would be a shame." I nodded my head, trying to ignore the lightheartedness. I felt the spit welling up in the corners of my mouth and I had to concentrate really hard not to drool. I had heard my mom say once that 'so-and-so was drooling all over him'. I had no idea that it could actually happen.

"I just want to spend some time with you, so you can be more comfortable around me. That and I miss you." When he said this, it sounded less of a statement and more like an excuse. He was feeling guilty and a little sad. Why?

"You don't want to go now? I feel like you're sorry you asked me?" I questioned, but as the words came out they didn't make sense to me.

"Don't be silly. I would go anywhere as long as you're there, too." His words were true. Why would he regret asking me when he obviously wanted to be with me?

"Have you wronged me in some way I am unaware of?" I asked.

"Do you trust me, Delia?" He asked grabbing my shoulders.

"Huh?" I was loosing my mind.

"Can you feel how much I care for you and know that I would never do anything to harm you?" He placed his hand on my cheek. Yes, I felt love though I wasn't ready to go there yet.

"Yes, I believe that you would never do anything to hurt me ever," I said.

"I ask you to remember this moment in the future when you get to know me better. I just hope then that you will understand."

"Understand what?" I wondered.

"Promise me, please?" He pushed.

"Ok, I promise," I shrugged.

"Good! Now let's go ride on the one of the fastest roller coasters in the world."

We stood in line for the The Heart Attack for an hour and a half. He had tricked me again because there is pretty much nothing else to do but talk except for a beach ball floating by to hit. We all laughed as an angry security guard ran through the lines trying to take away our only distraction from the smell of people.

It was a pretty October day with a light breeze
and warm sun. In seventeen seconds it was over, but the
exhilaration lasted for hours. Going three hundred fifty miles
an hour and four hundred feet up will definitely lighten
your mood.

We dashed around the park from one coaster to the
next easily, with the older rides having shorter lines. We
didn't break for even a drink until we were running from the
Mean Streak, which was properly named for the backbreaking
wooden coaster's ride, when I stopped short at what was in
front of me. The carnival music drifted from it, and as Lily's
carousel turned, so did my stomach.

"Are you okay?" I asked him, unsure with all the
emotions of the others walking by occupied my senses.

"Yeah. Do you want to go on it?"

"No, I don't do well with things that spin." I said
because I wanted to keep the carousel exactly as it should be to
him, as her carousel.

When I got home I put on Lily's Lyra. An old alert
message came up right away saying she had an appointment
with a Dr. H. Guardez at two thirty August 3.

The next day curiosity got the better of me. I called the
code in her contacts and found out Dr. Hannah Guardez was an
obstetrician. I asked the receptionist if they did gynecology
appointments too. She told me that Dr. Guardez specialized
only in obstetrics for teenagers. In less then a second, my
instincts to protect Gregory and Nola took over. There and then
I made a decision. They would never know how much they'd
really lost.

# CHAPTER 06

"Why are we here again?" I hissed in a whisper trying to keep my balance.

"To get you to try something new. Next week we are going to try a pottery class."

"I think I'm going to fall." I worried, not wanting to be the class's comic relief.

"Hold your stomach in, like the yoga teacher said."

"My stomach muscles are about to burst." I muttered.

"Then maybe you should stop talking and start focusing." Gregory said in his know-it-all fashion.

"How are you so good at this?" I glared.

"I'm not. I'm a runner and I have absolutely no flexibility at all. So calm down and let your mind quiet itself."

"I'm not sure how to do that," I growled.

"What if I told you in the loudest room you can disconnect and find silence?"

"I would say…SAY WHAT?" My voice grew louder than a whisper. The yoga teacher looked up at us and then chimed what looked like two little cymbals together.

"Imagine your eyes are telescopes and slowly lose focus on what is in front so that only your peripherals are clear. It helps to look up slightly. Then close your eyes and hear the sound of wind blowing past you. Blowing you up and away from your body till you are hovering looking down on it just as an observer."

"Ok." It was working. I was actually out of my body.

"Now listen to the instructor and do the next position not from here, but there." He instructed.

She did something called a downward facing dog with one leg extended. "Hey I did it." I smiled.

"Of course you did. Empaths can do more than just feel. They can create a place inside themselves, a shell that can be impenetrable to almost anyone."

"To almost anyone?" I asked confused.

"Well except to the one who is meant to love them." Gregory's eyes averted down.

I love you too, the self outside of me wanted to scream out, but I kept my mouth clamped shut and went back into downward dog. Biting down on my lower lip until the faint taste of blood arrived. I was still unable to tell him how I felt. Am I ready yet? I was also beginning to feel light headed holding downward dog, until the instructor chimed her magic fingers again, "alright class, now into upward dog, and breath in, and breath out." On my exhale I glanced over to admire his jawline arched into the air, beads of sweat running down his chiseled cheeks, yeah...Definitely not ready to tell him how I feel yet regarding love. Already back to being distracted by the lines and muscles of his forearms, I begin to fantasize how it would feel in their embrace.

The next few months flew by so fast because Gregory and Nola kept me busy. Gregory signed us both up for more classes at the community center. He said it was a good way of finding something I liked to do. I felt it was a good way for me to form closer bonds with him and Nola.

We took pottery, Tae Kwon Do, painting, photography and more yoga. We even joined a book club. Nola on the weekends taught me how to meditate. She said it was the only way to ground myself from the negativity surrounding me. When I didn't, everyone found out because I'd get really cranky. Gregory would immediately send me off for a 'time out'. He always caught it in time before I returned to my old sarcastic self.

Gregory had planned to take me to a nice restaurant for my birthday and after we would see Miss Saigon at the Playhouse. I was so excited that I glowed all week. Then Nola got a really bad cold and I insisted we stay home with her. Christmas was ten days away and I decided we could decorate a tree together and watch a Christmassy movie on screen.

We pulled out the old fake tree and decorations from the attic. I saw Gregory's face and wondered what was wrong when I found him staring at a small clay ornament on the floor that had fallen from its box. I touched his back and a picture of his sister hanging it on the tree last year popped into my head. I defused his pain through me until the memory brought a smile instead of a frown.

"You know she made this in sixth grade for Grandma. It took her forever in art class trying to get the eyes right." He held it up to the light. It was a Santa Claus whose eyes were slightly crossed. "Well, I guess she never did."

Not really knowing what to say, I nodded and rustled with a bunch of snarled up lights. He continued with, "Grandma wants me to go back to school in January so I can go to prom and graduation."

"Sounds like a good idea to me," I said.

"I don't know. I kind of like the freedom. Plus, it will be harder to be there without Lily."

"Whatever you want to do, but you know you might regret not facing this. Life without a senior year! It sounds like you'd be missing out on some important experiences to me. Good or bad, they're yours, and that's what helps you grow and move forward."

"Why thank you, Yoda." He was mocking me but he seemed to be considering it too. "Well, I guess I could give it a try," he conceded.

"Do or do not…" My voice sounded more like Kermit

the Frog and we both laughed hysterically. Then I saw them, first a few, then the whole tree. "Hey, I didn't see you put the twinkle lights on. You did that fast. I still haven't unsnarled this ball yet."

"Huh? What do you mean?" He got up and came towards me.

"The tree is covered with lights. Hey, they're moving. Of course you have some sort of fancy kind. Are they the bubble lights?"

"Delia," his voice sounded upset and he gestured to the tree. "There are absolutely no lights on that tree!"

He took my hand and I felt fear radiate from his heart to mine then a picture of a woman in her forties flashed in my head.

"Who is that in your mind?" I asked.

"My mother!" He growled. He took me back downstairs and sat me down on the couch. He put his face in mine looking directly into my eyes...

"Gregory what is going on?" I asked quietly so not to disturb Nola.

"Grandma, can you come here please?" He yelled across the house. I noticed now the twinkle lights were all over this room, too.

"Shush, what is the matter with you? You'll upset her with your yelling. Maybe she is asleep." I said in a motherly tone.

"What is it dear?" Nola appeared from the other room.

"Delia is having optical migraines." He said very nervous.

"Are you sure?" She asked sharply.

"Wow! When did you decorate this room with twinkle lights Nola? You're supposed to be resting."

"You're seeing lights dear?" She said in a calm tone but stood very still.

"Yes, don't you?" She sat next to me and held my hand.

I felt fear and I saw the same image of Gregory's mother as before.

"Please will someone tell me what is going on? And what are optical migraines?"

Nola answered with a hoarse voice, her cold taking its toll. "That is a term that neurologists use for seeing lights that aren't there, at least to them. It is what happens when the veil of this world lifts and you will see glimpses of the next. Only the most powerful of Psychics can see them. My daughter is one."

"Cool, I'm Psychic, too. That will probably be more fun than feeling pain! You said the next world. Do you mean heaven?" What a neat birthday present! I thought.

Gregory completely ignored the last question. "No this isn't cool, Delia. There are very few Psychics who are this powerful and there are no known Psychic Empaths that don't need to be institutionalized." His mother popped back into my head. "My mother was just a Psychic until she turned twenty-seven and then she became an Empath. She was not only now seeing the world's pain but she felt it with every vision. Unable to help those in a hurricane before, now she felt their fear as they died. Seeing the lights is one of the first signs of being a Mentalist."

"Interesting title, kind of a play on words especially when you're committed," I tried to lighten his mood.

"This is not a joke!" He was freaking out.

"Your mom was older than me and I'm sure it didn't help that your dad freaked and left her. I have support and I feel fine right now. Please, let's not jump to any conclusions."

"She could be right, Greggy." Nola put a hand on his shoulder.

"Yeah, Greggy relax," I said.

He glared at me. Then a smile came across his frustrated face. "For that little comment, you won't be getting your birthday present."

"That's not fair." I whined.

I started riffling through his pockets and then I ran up to his room. It was on his desk nicely wrapped with a silver bow. I reached for it but he was too fast and snatched it first.

"Let me have it?" I whined.

I had never been given a present from a boy and I was dying to know what it is. The box was small so it must have been jewelry. He handed it too me and inside was a gold ring with my birthstone in it. It was engraved inside the band and read "Gra anois agus go deo".

As I read it out loud he said, "It's Gaelic, it means love now and forever." I immediately kissed him and then ran down stairs to show Nola.

We spent my whole Christmas break together. Gregory watched me like a hawk while Nola was also on my back to meditate. She gave me lessons on being Psychic, on what to do when this happens or that. The two of them drove me nuts and I was glad to be getting back to school soon. I talked Gregory into going back to school, also by saying our schools were closer than his house from my school. If I had a problem, he could reach me faster. It really was a matter of three to five minutes, but he liked the idea and I was happy to see him getting back into a routine.

When someone dies, most of the time people can't handle it. Your friends kind of drop off because you're not the same person in grief. It happened to me when my dad died and it was the same for Gregory. He really had no reason to go back after the accident. He was so depressed in the summer that Nola thought it was best for him to be home schooled during part of the fall. I don't think she was expecting him to get used to it the way he did.

We had been back for about a week since break. I walked over to his school and waited outside like I always did. Then the wind picked up and my ears were about to freeze off so I walked inside. The bell rang and everyone was exiting the classrooms to go home. I walked up and down the halls for a few minutes looking for him and then I saw him leaning with his back against his locker. Everyone started to disperse and as I got closer I saw her. She was leaning up against him and her hand was reaching up to touch his hair. He saw me and quickly pushed her away looking ashamed. I sped up and heard him trying to introduce me but I didn't care. I had to know.

I grabbed his hand with my one hand and hers in my other.

"What is she doing, Gregory?" I heard the slut ask.

"Delia, no!" Gregory shouted.

And then I saw them in my mind but everything was a hazy red. Red meant the past. I think. Well I was hoping because she and Gregory were in the back of his Vapor doing it. Damn it! Why couldn't I remember what Nola had taught me? The color red meant the past, green was present, and bright white was the future right? I was so confused.

Gregory and I never talked about sex because I just assumed we were both virgins. 'How could I be so stupid?' I thought. He was always so confident about that stuff when we made out. Then I realized he knew what he was doing.

"Delia, please?" I heard him softly say in my left ear. He was doing it again, lulling me into submission. "Let go of her, love." He was now prying my hand from hers.

"But he is meant for me." I heard my lips say as I felt my head tip slightly sideway like a confused puppy-dog.

"Yes, yes I am. Now let us go somewhere less conspicuous and talk." He said very softly. Then he said harshly, "Goodbye, Candy."

"Wait a second, her name is Candy?" I said in a hysterical voice.

I started to laugh like someone losing it. Hell, I was loosing it. The slut's name was Candy. How perfect! I wasn't mad at him at all, which I thought was a bit weird. But I wanted to kill her. I wanted to take her life energy from her body. I saw everything in a vision of a strobe light. First I was grabbing for her. Then her forehead was against mine and it was happening. I was killing her.

"Delia, stop it now!" Gregory had his arms around the outside of mine and pulled me away. Candy was on the ground now gasping for air but he wasn't worried about her. He was worried about me. I felt it and I took great satisfaction in that. "I think it would be best if you stayed away from me from now on, Candy." He was still restraining me. "Now go home and lie down. You have been feeling sick all day."

"Yes, of course." She turned and walked away from us.

He walked me to the Vapor while I stayed in a daze. What had I just done and what has he been doing with her? The daze slowly wore off and I was thinking clearly.

"Gregory? What just happened back there?" I was starting to cry when we pulled into his driveway.

"What did you exactly see Delia?"

"I saw you having sex with… Candy…in here." I made sure I put an emphasis on her name. I wanted to sound snotty. Suddenly I wanted to get out of the vehicle. As far as I was concerned it had her all over it. I ran into the house and assumed Nola was napping when she wasn't there to greet us.

"You are getting it all wrong." He looked scared. He obviously didn't want me to know about her.

"Did you have sex with her?" I pointed my finger into his chest.

"Yes, yes I did. It happened once right after Lily died. She had always had a thing for me. She came here with a casserole and we started talking. I was waiting for you for so long I deluded myself into thinking she was you. We had sex in my Vapor and then that was the end of it. I guess she had me and that was enough for her. Well, until today, that is."

"And what did I do to her?"

"You stole her energy from her. I told you that Mentalists are powerful."

"Why did I try to kill her?"

"I guess jealousy got the best of you. If you are scared or hurt, your abilities take over. There is no right or wrong to it, all it knows is what you're meant to do."

"I am not meant to kill anyone." I was spinning out of control again.

"I know that. You will know what is right or wrong by controlling them one day. You will feel it inside. Though we are still young and sometimes let our emotions rule, as you can see what happened with Candy."

"Whatever!" I was crying harder now. It infuriated me he said her name again.

"Go and meditate, Delia. You have been around all those negative emotions at school today." He placed his hands on my cheeks and he kissed me ever so lightly. I was feeling the daze fill me up again. I wanted to do whatever he wanted now. Then his voice was soft again. "I love you so much. Please don't go home mad at me. Go and meditate. We can talk when you calm down." He was using extra force on the last sentence to get what he wanted. I could feel it and I was hopeless to his words.

"Okay," I said. As I walked off like a spoiled child, I called behind me, "I can't control myself right now, but when I'm done, we have some talking to do."

I'd seen him use his ability now with Candy. I now know how it worked. When I wasn't so weak to his will I was going to let him have it.

I found him when I was done on the beach. He was standing looking at the frozen lake. I stood next to him and waited for him to start.

"Are you going to break up with me?" he asked.

"Why would you think that?"

He shrugged and answered, "Everyone in my life except Grandma has left me. I was wondering if you would do the same. My ability will never stop the people I love from leaving."

*Ha! He does have one.* I knew it. I thought.

"Why did you lie about your ability that day last fall?"

"I never lied. I just said that I'm not special because I'm not. I don't have a specific purpose like you and like Lily was supposed to."

"How can you say that? Nola saw you and me together in her dreams. Together, which means you are very important part of me following this destiny or whatever this is. Look you stopped me from killing Candy today. You have taught, protected and loved me the past three months even when I pushed you away. We are meant to be together. I haven't told you this because it is really hard for me. I kind of thought you already knew but if you thinking I could leave you your wrong."

He wasn't looking at me. He sighed and said, "I don't want you to feel stuck with me because it is your destiny. You don't need me to get there."

I had to find a way to prove this to him. I turned him to look at me and put my forehead to his and my hands on his face.

"Aren't you listening silly boy?" Then I focused really hard and said, "I love you Gregory with all my soul has in it." I was doing the same thing I did with Candy except instead of taking, this time I was giving. "I want to be with you forever. Even if I die, I will never leave you. Nothing will take me away from you."

It was starting to hurt giving him all I could, but I didn't care. I was going to die proving this to him if I had to.

"Delia, you need to stop." I ignored him. I wanted to make my point. I wouldn't stop until I blacked out. "Delia, I believe you. I want you to stop this."

He was using his ability but it wasn't working with me. I was using pure love. His hand cupped my chin and then he kissed me. We were standing in twenty-eight degree weather and I was burning up. Sweat was starting to drip down my face.

Then I saw it. The light between us, our souls were connecting. This was my wedding day and I was wearing a huge ski jacket and snow boots.

*I bet Candy never did this with him*, I thought smugly.

I pulled away slowly completely out of breath.

"I guess we belong to each other now." I said in a soft voice.

"Forever, love, forever." He smiled.

We walked together hand in hand ready for our future yet my words haunted me.

*Even if I die I will never leave you. Nothing can take me away from you.*

# CHAPTER 07

The school day had been exceptionally long one on February 13th. There was a motivational speaker that made me want to take a nap and then my history teacher showed us a movie.

Things had changed so much. My mom happily said I was a different person. Though I still didn't have a favorite color yet and I didn't have a single friend to speak of besides Gregory and Nola.

I ate lunch alone everyday. This didn't bother me before because I didn't know what to do with those feelings that people threw at me, but now I felt something was missing. I needed someone my age to be girly with that understood me like Gregory. Maybe I was asking too much from the universe.

Gregory never hung out with other guys. He told me this was because he could never be himself and talk about me or what set us apart. It didn't seem to bother him.

I was different and it was like the others knew it. I wondered if any of them even knew my name. All the groups we joined at the community center helped me to determine the things I thought were fun, but even in the book club, the others were older and not interested in talking about anything but the book for that month.

I was beginning to feel a missing link in my chain. I have never had a best friend except for Gregory and he didn't want to go prom dress shopping with me. My mom was always at work or out with her new boyfriend. So I was going alone and I was in tears. I didn't know what to buy; the only dress I owned was the one I wore to my dad's funeral and that was almost four years ago. Then I thought of something. Maybe I could encourage someone to help me by using my ability, if I could see something and manipulate them into a conversation with some inside knowledge.

This is pathetic, I thought.

I sat there in the mall and watched as different groups of teenagers walked back and forth. There were the Goth chicks but I wasn't into the style. There were the jock girls whose muscles made me feel inferior. Then there was the pretty girls, loaded with make-up that slightly had the look of hookers with their cheerleading sports bras, tight mini-skirts and prostitute pink lipstick.

I gave up and walked into the most expensive store in the mall. The first tag I read said fifteen hundred dollars. I walked back out because I didn't have a job and my mother gave me a five hundred dollar limit on my clip account.

I followed a few people my age until I saw a woman about twenty years old, go into a store with prom dresses in the front. Perfect, I thought. Then I lost her once inside.

Getting discouraged and about to give up, I went from aisle to aisle of dresses, running my hands along them. Black was formal norm, but it was a spring dance...shouldn't I wear something bright or light colored, though I knew white was too much. I didn't want to look like we were getting married (although we practically were). I turned to leave and there she was, the woman I had followed, staring at me.

"Can I help you find something?" she said with an open smile. She wore a pendant around her neck that was a ring of charms. When she came closer I saw that they were the sun, the moon and a star.

"Um, do you work here?" I asked, stupidly stunned.

She tapped her name tag that read Melanie and I was,

now, officially embarrassed.

"Are you going to prom?" She smiled again.

"Yeah and I don't know what I'm doing." I never even thought to let a sales person help me. I was so used to everything being a challenge. I guess I turned this into something harder than it was. Maybe I let my loneliness get the better of me.

"Oh well, sometimes, we make things harder than they seem." She just repeated my thoughts to me.

How odd, I thought.

Maybe she has an ability like me and we could be the best of friends, I dreamed. I could get a job here to get to know her.

You are crazy, I told myself. Even if you did know something about clothes, things don't work that way. You're setting yourself up for disappointment.

"Hey, do you need a job by any chance? I had someone quit yesterday and I'm in desperate need." She asked and smiled an even wider smile than before.

"Um, like I said, I really don't know anything about clothes." I wondered if she knows she's a telepath, I thought.

"Yes, yes I do." She answered the question in my thoughts so nonchalant it made me laugh. Nola had told me about all the different ways to be psychic and telepathy was intriguing to me but not an ability I wanted.

She continued "So about the job. You do know something about clothes. Look at how you put together that top with those slacks. It's casual, yet very classy."

"Thanks, but I don't think so."

"Oh, I can teach you anything you don't know, silly. Gosh, I never had to convince someone to take a job before. You really do make everything hard, don't you?" She tilted her head to the side, squinting her eyes. She was as tall as Gregory and so slim that I almost hated her. Her hair was awesome. Like Gregory's, it was incredibly bright blond that had an abundance of ringlet curls.

"Thanks, but it's from a bottle and the curls drive me crazy." She responded to my last thought again.

She wanted me to know she was a telepath. Why?

"I thought I was the one following you, but you read my thoughts and followed me didn't you?" I asked.

"Yes." She said so honestly it was amazing.

"Oh, you must think I'm pretty pathetic." I stated without sadness. I liked my life, I just wanted a little more.

"No, it's hard to make friends in our situation. Having an ability can turn people off because we sometimes tell them things they don't want to hear accidentally. We are what we are. If we hide it, we don't follow the path set for us, we'll just wilt and eventually die." She was right. I felt like I was dying before I met Gregory and he explained what was happening.

"Ooooooo…who's Gregory?" Her eyes were wide with wonder, but three new customers came in the door at the same time. So she walked away calling behind her, "Well you can tell me if you want the job tomorrow after school.
See you then."

I watched for a moment and then put the dress I was holding back. I walked away mystified.

*I guess I have a job or she gave me till tomorrow to decide, I think.*

I went home thinking a long time about everything that had happened. Gregory called and I told him. He just laughed saying, "Only you would go dress shopping and come home with a job. You just made work out of something that, for a girl, is supposed to be fun." I hung up with him a little miffed but he was technically right.

I was looking forward to tomorrow. Learning something new and meeting different kinds of people was exciting. Whether I could help them was a mystery because I really didn't have any skills per se, except what Nola and Gregory taught me and I don't see myself as becoming a fortuneteller as a job prospect. Though, I haven't been able to see the future, only the past, so it would be a short read anyway. I could see myself telling some poor soul that their husband was cheating and not knowing what was going to happen next. *Will they work it out? I don't know because I only see the past.* It was probably best that I didn't see the future. It might drive me insane the way it did to Gregory's poor mother.

After school, Gregory drove me back to the mall. "I am going to miss not seeing you everyday. I might have to get a job, too, so I will be distracted." He kissed up my neck all the way to my mouth where he lingered until I shoved him.

"You are so bad. Now let me go. I want to grab a drink on the way." And he did but with a quick kiss. He knew I was excited and was stalling on purpose.

Melanie was at the front counter and smiled when she saw me. "How is my new employee today?"

"Fine, thank you and you?" I said feeling awkward.

"Great! Now that you're here." She seemed so sure that I could do the job but the excitement was quickly turning to fear. "Oh, don't be afraid." She read my thoughts again. "By the way, what name should I write at the top of your timecard?" Boy did she have faith. She just hired someone who forgot to introduce herself.

"Oh, sorry. My name is Delia Stanton." I had a timecard!

"Pleased to officially meet you, Delia. If you come on time, take your breaks, and help every customer you see, we'll be friends for life," she said.

"I got it." I said although I had a lot to learn still.

"Yes, you do."

I found that I didn't mind at all her reading my thoughts. It was kind of a comfort not having to be someone I'm not, so giving her the same courtesy was easy. Even my mom didn't know yet or maybe she didn't want to know.

All in all, the day I would say was a success. Though

we never had time to talk and I had so many questions for her. They would have to wait because Gregory was coming to pick me up.

As I was leaving, she called after me. "Tomorrow you are going to tell me about this Gregory."

"Definitely. See you tomorrow." I said before I walked out the door.

As Gregory drove me home, I rattled off my first day of work. Then when we got to my house he stayed quiet for a minute with a face solemn.

"What's wrong?"

"I just realized that it's April second today and my mother's birthday is on the twentieth. I usually visit her on her birthday. And um, I was wondering if it would be a good idea to bring you. She won't even know we are there, but I still make the effort every year. My Grandma found a really nice place in Miami, Florida. Would you want to go with Grandma and me?"

"Yes, I would love to go, but I don't know what my mom will think."

He smiled a wide smile and then said, "Just let me ask her and she'll say yes within five minutes."

"Oh I forgot you're the perfect son she always wanted because you TOLD her to love you!" I rolled my eyes. His ability was so unfair.

"Yes, and she will be tired right now after work, a perfect time to strike." He started to rub his hands together deviously.

"You are so scary." I said then quickly asked, "Does it work all the time?" I was very curious.

"No, not if the person has their head clear. It works the best when the person is weak or distracted, with anger or sadness. Also, when a person is a dim wit, it works almost always." He said very proud of himself, so I couldn't resist commenting.

"You mean like *Candy*," I said her name in a snotty way like I always did. He just looked at me, but I read yes on his face.

He did his magic on my mom and she said yes before he could finish his question. He kissed me lightly and promptly left quite happy with himself.

I meditated and went to bed. The dreams that night were vivid in a haze of bright white. I was walking down a long hallway there were doors on both sides with square windows. As I went to look into the first, a face popped up on the other side. It was a very large man and he was yelling at me. The yelling was muffled and I couldn't understand him. I backed away and started looking into all the windows until I was able to see her again. It was Gregory's mother sitting on a bed rocking back and forth. I tried the door, but it was locked, then I searched my pockets and found an old metal key in my left side. It was the size of my hand. It slid nicely in and I walked in thinking she couldn't see me, but she grabbed my hands and pulled me down to her level. I was looking straight into her eyes, which were wild with insanity.

"You," she yelled, "You have something that belongs to me!" Then I woke up very disturbed and not having a clue what to do with the warning.

I sat at the front window the next day worried about how to act around Gregory. I decided not to tell him. I knew keeping a secret from someone you love could be impossible. When his truck pulled up to take me to work my heart almost stopped. I walked slowly and opened the Vapor's door casually.

He was laughing and said, "Hey Miss Easy Going. Do you want to close the front door?" I looked back and he was right - the front door to the house was wide open because I was focusing on not looking hasty. I hastily didn't close and lock it.

"Ugh." I growled and placed my clip around my right hand forefinger on the pad next to the door. When I climbed back into the Vapor he pestered me the whole ride. I kept my very obvious mouth shut. I kissed him quick and bolted from the car when we got to the mall, which probably made things worse.

"Hi, Melanie. How's it going?" I asked her quickly in a really high voice.

"Great! You seem awfully hyper today?" *Damn, I really don't want to talk about it.*

"Oh you really must now!" I glowered at her response to my thoughts.

"I just had a dream about Gregory's mom last night and I'm supposed to meet her in two weeks. Oh by the way, I'm going to need to have a few days off around the seventeenth. I'll let you know when I get the plane tickets." I was being sassy on purpose. I trying to bait her so she wouldn't ask questions about the dream.

"Don't you have some nerve newbie asking for days off, but if I did, say give you the time off. Where would you be going?" She was playing coy asserting herself in her humorous way. I knew she was dying to get more info on Gregory and my relationship.

"Do you think there will be nice weather in South Carolina in the Coastal district? Oh, I think I might buy a new bathing suit just in case." I poised my finger up to my smiling lips in a thinking pose. The bragging was fun, because normally, my life was nothing to boast about. She took it in stride and let me play my little game.

"That is so unfair you little wench. The weatherman today said it was going to keep snowing until the end of the month. Why do you get a vacation from Jack Frost, when I get to suffer?" She pretended to pout as she threw a pair of indigo pants at me subtly telling me to get to work and start folding.

"Just for that I get to take you shopping. We should go downtown. They always have the best spring lines. We could find you the tiniest bikini at this one store I know."

"I don't think I'm ready to have Gregory see me in a bikini, though I could use a couple nice shirts and maybe a sundress."

She smiled at me with a slight evil that made me think she was going to get her way anyways. We decide on tomorrow, simply because she was so excited to shop and I was happy to have someone to finally shop with. Maybe I could even get that prom dress I would need in less than two months. Gregory picked me up later and I had my first official paycheck in my hand, which I waved at him ecstatically.

"Look at you!" He smiled.

"I know! I feel empowered. Melanie wants to go downtown tomorrow morning, so can we go to the movies in the late afternoon."

"This Melanie sees you more than I have lately. I'm not sure I want to share you." He smiled putting his arm around my shoulder and pulled my body towards him kissing the top of my head. "Would it be too much to ask if I could go with?"

The guilt was rising up inside me and making my throat tighten. How do I tell the man I love that I don't want him to go because it was official 'girl time'? I was so unsure the indecision was making me sad. I didn't want to hurt him, but I didn't want to be begging for my own personal freedom. Right now Nola and I were all he had because he really didn't care to socialize at school since Lily died. I took a deep breath and reached for his hand. *I would just say what was in my heart and see what happens.*

"I don't think that's a good idea. She might feel like a third wheel and she has been so nice. I wouldn't want her feeling alienated. Plus, I was also going to look for a prom dress and I kind of like it to be a surprise." I waited for my rejection to settle in his thoughts. That was hard to say because I was so afraid he might think I didn't love him. Maybe by telling him the truth…I was loving him. I hoped he saw it that way.

*Is honesty a form of love?* I wondered.

"Well, I get to pick the movie then." Gregory smiled

and that was it.

I learned then and there that understanding was a form of love too. My heart started racing and I pulled his face to mine. When we stopped kissing, he put the truck in drive and took me home both of us knowing that in those ten minutes our relationship had grown a little closer that night.

Melanie picked me up in her red Saturn and we headed east on I-90. We sang the songs on the radio and laughed at our made up words for lyrics until I saw the Terminal Tower district and I started to get a strange tingling feeling at the top of my head. Melanie was getting off the exit ramp but it wasn't the Cleveland I knew. Everything was spread out and there was a smell of industry that I didn't remember. She pulled up to the parking garage but to me we were hanging in mid air and there was nothing below us. I was unsure what was happening, but Melanie didn't seem to think anything was wrong, so it had to be just me.

As I got out of the car, it disappeared, and I was left hanging about one hundred feet in the air. I followed Melanie to what must have been an escalator up to the main mall area of what I could remember. When we got to the top, Melanie walked through a wall that I didn't remember being there. I knew the mall was on the other side. I couldn't follow her even though I wanted to. The wall wouldn't let me through. I turned and decided to go outside and around the exterior of the Terminal Tower. I saw only two people in the whole city so it seemed tagging along was the only way to get back. Because apparently this wasn't my time.

# CHAPTER 08

**Cleveland Great Lakes Exposition (World's Fair)**
**Saturday July 3, 1937**

I watched them walk hand in hand knowing that they were just an imprint of what happened once. Though, these were ghosts of the past, I wondered if I could touch them, but didn't dare. They could disappear as fast as I dreamed them up and this was so fascinating I didn't want to leave yet.

I was in awe of the sights. In front of me read a sign: Bridge of Great Lakes Presidents. As we walked across it every hundred so feet there were humongous golden eagles spreading their wings with a copper penny and a particular president on the side of its base. Music was coming from all angles. I watched a man walk by playing an accordion while oddly dressed dancers wearing wooden shoes clipped-clopped as they trotted by. Though there was excitement at every corner, my ghosts were not even noticing the beauty surrounding them. In fact, they were fighting.

"What do you want from me Juniper? I can still taste the blood in my mouth. You know, he likes to lick his victims. He is a heathen and he is here right now. He killed last night you know, then threw the body in the river by the Flats. I went to the police already in June and Eliot Ness wouldn't even see me. Now today, on my Saturday off, I bump into the murder, here, when I was having such a good time. I can't even enjoy the last season of the centennial. Juniper, I want to leave now!"

The one talking withdrew her hand and Juniper turned to face her hostile companion. Juniper had her hand on her very pregnant belly and was tapping her toe. I could tell she was holding in her temper.

"Don't you think I haven't seen the same Torso Murderer visions as you Helen? You have to learn to accept the good with the bad. We must do what we can but we can't force others to listen. You know this. You will have visions everywhere. What are you going to do? Lock yourself away in that tiny apartment with your mother barking orders at you for the rest of your life. Life is meant to be lived." Juniper ghost said.

"It always comes to my tiny apartment. Maybe I'll marry Ronny Chase just so you can't flaunt your big house on the lake in my face anymore," Helen's ghost stated.

"Helen, that is not what I meant. You have to move out and live your life. Come live with James and me, we would love it. If you marry that cold fish, it will be the biggest mistake of your life. Your mother and Chase don't accept us for who we are. They think it is the work of the devil. You are creating a cage of your own making," Juniper huffed.

"You can't talk to me about this when you have everything: a nice house, a great husband, a baby on the way and money in the bank, something pretty much no one has these days. In the crash we lost the steel mill, our fortune, our status and my father who couldn't take failure. I am not getting any younger and a rich man wants to marry me. I'm going to listen to my mother. We have a ticket to getting everything we lost back and I'm going to take it," Helen shouted.

"We…who is this *we*?" Juniper opened her arms palms up in a questioning gesture. "You need to do what is right for you, and this is not it. You and I have been friends since age three. Please listen to me. This isn't going to work."

Right then I saw something twitch on Juniper's face. Water started then gushed down her legs.

She continued her body hunch over, "Okay Helen, I think I'm ready to go home now."

"Oh my goodness, is it time? Here take my arm we have to get you to a taxi."

Everything faded and buildings rose up around me where there were booths and exhibits. I found myself in the middle of 9th Street with a delivery shuttle stopping dead almost running me over. In shock, I fell to the ground. I felt a hand take hold of me and help me up. It was Melanie and I let her usher me to the side of the road.

"Oh, I'm so sorry you got away from me. You know, you're awfully quick."

"I don't even get what happen and you are acting like you know the whole story." I said still in a daze.

"I do. I saw everything. That vision was amazing. Do you get those all the time?"

"No, and you are so incredibly freaky. So what was I doing?"

"You just meandered around the city and I did my best to keep you safe without interfering." She smiled.

It amazed me that her smile was genuine and she was having fun. I was glad because anyone else would have left me not knowing what I was doing. Today of all days I was grateful for our newfound friendship.

It amazed me that her smile was genuine and she was having fun. I was glad because anyone else would have left me not knowing what I was doing. Today of all days I was grateful for our newfound friendship.

When I arrived at Gregory's and Nola's, I was not sure where to begin to tell them my adventures in the city. Little did I know my time traveling was not over. As soon as I walked through the door, the haze of red engulfed me, and I knew there was more to Helen and Juniper's story. I followed a maid carrying a tray up the stairs and to the open master bedroom door. Juniper was in bed with a huge smile holding a baby in her arms. Helen stood at the edge of the bed; her eyes said more than her smile. I could hear the radio concluding some show called Guiding Light and a song by Bing Crosby was being announced.

"Are you sure you don't want to go to the hospital?" Helen asked nervously.

"Don't be silly, Helen. The doctor is coming today. Besides, Nola and I are fine." I realized that she was talking about Gregory's Grandma, Nola. Juniper was looking lovingly at her baby.

"I am only being realistic. Most people of wealth or poverty have their babies in hospitals now you know."

"My midwife was wonderful. Besides, what could happen to her? Nola is the first of The Alignment and is thus protected by the prophecy."

"Life isn't like a soap opera or a movie you see, Juniper. This isn't Topper and James isn't Cary Grant. People do die and are dying out there in the world you don't live in. We aren't kids anymore writing down prophecies in a secret journal. You have a baby now and need to bring yourself into this reality."

"Where is your faith, Helen Bracken? You have been hanging around too many negative people like Ronny Chase."

"I accepted his proposal, Juniper."

"Helen, you can't be serious!"

"Yes, and he had one condition…if I want mother to move in with us."

"And what is this bellowing condition?" Juniper hissed through her teeth. I could tell, Juniper hated Ronny Chase's arrogance, controlling her dear friend.

"Only, I'm not to associate with certain people of a questionable nature that could harm his reputation." Helen looked down at the floor.

"Did he name any names or do I need to guess that James and I are at the top of that list because of our eccentricities and lack of church attendance." Tears were streaming down her face with every word.

"Well, I told him that you believed in God."

"Why thank you for defending me, but I can take care of myself and my Nola. As for James, God help Ronny if the two of them meet on the street. James won't take kindly to your corruption." Nola started to cry and there was sudden static in the air that made the old standup radio loose its reception.

"Please, Juniper, I'm sure I could sneak over on occasion."

"Don't bother." Her voice cracked. "I can't be friends with someone who is turning her back on everything she truly believed and sees from visions. It all comes from somewhere, Helen. You are throwing yourself off track and I can't watch you destroy yourself. You won't produce a child for the Alignment with this loveless marriage."

"I don't want this cursed gift anymore. I don't like knowing the future. No one wants to hear that Amelia Earhart is lost and will never be found before it hits the newspapers. There is no Alignment, only those who have means and those who don't. I can only believe in common sense from now on."

Helen turned walked through the door and Juniper said these final words, "Fine you fool, but even heaven won't help you if you don't guide a child of the Alignment when you encounter one." With that, the haze was gone and I was standing in Nola's bedroom by myself.

I went downstairs to find Nola and Gregory at the kitchen table and when Nola looked at me, my hands began to shake. All I could see was that baby, well her actually, and time had no meaning to me anymore.

"Nola, are you a child of the Alignment?"

"Yes Delia, I believe I am." Her eyes showed no surprise.

"Am I one also?" I really didn't want the answer, but I was being pulled to find out what they had hidden from me since the beginning.

"Gregory and you were the last two to be born for the prophecy. Their journals showed me that it was true. Well, when you showed up at the beach, at least, I knew that you were the youngest and last."

"You had your doubts, then, about your mother's and my Great Aunt Helen's predictions."

I couldn't face the word 'prophecy'. It seemed too overwhelming to handle. Gregory got up and led me to sit at the table with them but my legs wouldn't bend into position because fear was rising inside me. I wanted to bolt and run away. He made a shushing sound in my ear like a mother would calm her child. My legs responded and released. I was so ridged that I felt like a folding chair.

*His little Barbie Doll, is that what I was? Who did he think he was, keeping this from me? Maybe he didn't love me after all. I knew the two of them less than a year. Who were they to me?* My thoughts twisted in my head.

"Who are you people? All this talk of a prophecy like it's some sort of doomsday cult. Wonderful!" I said and stood up from where Gregory placed me.

"Don't do this Delia, you're just scared and filled with the city's negativity. Think of all the people you bumped into there. Please think about it logically."

He was pushing me with his mind, to talk this out, but I didn't want to. I just wanted to leave.

*Great Aunt Helen thought Juniper was crazy. Maybe her descendants were just as nuts.*

"I'm leaving and don't try to stop me!" I was wagging my finger at both of them when I turned and ran. The words coming out of my mouth didn't even seem like my own, they were harsh and throaty.

I grabbed Gregory's Vapor key to have them in my hand to put them into the ignition. When I made it outside, Gregory tackled me to the ground and I sat up. We were both kneeling and he pinned my arms down with a bear hug from behind so

I couldn't get away.

"STOP AND LISTEN TO ME!" His voice echoed in my ears as he put his mind inside mine.

My body went limp into his arms and then the pain came, his pain. It radiated up my arms through me. I saw images of his sister crying and running to an old four wheel car as Gregory followed. He was reliving the night she died through me. I could hear him crying in my hair. His whimpers released any anger I held towards him for not telling me the truth. He thought I wasn't mature enough to face it. He was right, obviously as I so nicely demonstrated and to my embarrassment, in front of Nola a minute ago.

"It's not your fault she died." I turned myself facing him as I ran my fingers through his hair.

"She told me she was pregnant and I started yelling at her. I called her stupid and irresponsible. I made her so upset she sped off in her car to get away from me. The rain earlier had made the asphalt oily and slick. When she turned onto Basset Road she was going fifty into a pole with no seatbelt in that piece of crap death machine. She didn't have a chance when the paramedics got there. If I had just understood, if I had just been there for her. Instead I called her a slut."

Gregory's pain did something to me. It was real. My hysteria wasn't. There was a flip or a snap. I realized I was in control of the light and dark. My tool or sword of choice was compassion and I could wield it. I controlled how I saw things.

"So when I met you on the beach that day it wasn't only grief, but guilt on top of your grief. That is why you couldn't heal without me releasing you from your guilt. Don't you see, I could have chosen any boat that day. You brought me here. Otherwise, I wouldn't have come. It was you, Gregory. It has always been you. Everything is as it should be. Her death was senseless and there is nothing you can do to change it. All we can do is be grateful for what we do have right now. She doesn't blame you, hell she probably brought me to you so you could heal."

"You can't be sure of that," was his only response.

We laid there in the front yard until I realized I owed Nola an apology. I took Gregory's hand and led him back into the house. She was at the table still reading a book like there hadn't been a temper tantrum recently in the room.

"I'm really sorry, Nola. I guess Gregory and you had your reasons for not telling me." *Like freak out irrationally…*

"We just wanted you to have a childhood for a little longer." Nola sighed.

"Please tell me what the prophecy is about. I want to know what the Alignment is."

"The Alignment of Kairos is a prophecy of hope. We all have our lives ruled by Chronos time, the clock on the wall or watch that tells us when we eat, sleep, and wake up. Kairos is the spirit's time to shine or the universe's way of letting you know you're in the right place at the right time. You might have had that feeling when you met Gregory. Juniper and Helen predicted a leader who will find others with her same talents. They will come together and enlighten the world to live differently. You are on your path Delia, but there are so many that stray and are lost. You saw this with Helen today. Your father's Great Aunt Helen to be exact. She was taken in by a Soul Shifter. Ronny Chase was a powerful creature."

"You know what happened in the city today." I was all geared up to tell my story.

"I took a nap and had a very interesting dream. I was with you the whole time. I'm just glad Melanie didn't let you get hit by that supply shuttle."

"Why is it so hard for me to control my emotions?" I was flushing red, remembering my bad behavior.

"Everyone has a stress threshold. You were exposed to a lot today and it's easy to handle in little increments, but with your empathic ability, there is only so much you can take to stay sane. Meltdowns are your body's way to let you know you have had enough. You need to take care of yourself, to protect yourself through meditation, exercise and a balanced diet. If you don't, you could become a Soul Shifter, too."

"I can tear people off their path? I can hurt people?" I sucked in the words not believing them.

"Everyone has a switch inside them, Delia. Emotional triggers bring about choices that hurt others. You saw that with Lily and Gregory."

"You can't blame him. It's not his fault."

"You misunderstand me. My granddaughter made an emotional choice during a party. When Gregory found out, he worried about his future (never meeting you to be exact) and made an emotional choice to spur Lily. It changed her path. Lily and Gregory are both responsible for her death."

*No* wonder Gregory felt so guilty. It's in the family genes. Even if I didn't believe in what Nola thought, I needed to move on. I had burning questions I need answered.

"How do I fulfill this prophecy? I mean are there instructions in Juniper and Helen's journals?"

"I only have one journal. The rest are missing. My mother told me that they would be seen when needed. I wouldn't worry. When the time is right, you will know what to do."

"No pressure, right? Are you sure you have the right girl?" I was kidding, but Gregory grabbed my hand still worried about my reaction.

"You are definitely the right person, trust me." Nola patted my cheek.

She knew because she has seen the future, and her confidence in me was unwavering. I still needed convincing; after all, I was just one girl.

# CHAPTER 09

Melanie found me some really nice sundresses when the store got its spring line that week. I found at the bottom of my bag a tiny bikini I vowed to return when I got back. I was so excited I couldn't sleep which is a really bad idea to do if you are traveling. Gregory had his eye on me, following behind me as I dropped important items like my ear clip between train changes. We weren't going to visit his mom till the next day, so we stopped at the hotel so I could take a shower and change before I did my mother a favor. Her one condition that she had for me going to Miami was that I visit my dad's sister, my Aunt Lisa, and her family. I was a little nervous considering I hadn't seen them since the funeral.

The only thing I remember of my cousin Kelly was her asking me, as I stared at my dad's closed casket, "Cancer's hereditary isn't it?" Thus we weren't the closest family members. It seemed to be a design lately that I face all of my least favorite memories as if I was cleaning all the cobwebs out of my brain. What was going to occupy my clutter-free mind was up to the great beyond.

"Oh, Dee Dee, there you are!" My Aunt said in somewhat of a baby voice while she stood holding open her hot pink door. She still treats me as if I'm a breastfeeding two year old. "You remember Kelly and this is her fiancé, Doug Walsh." Then she whispered like he couldn't hear, "He is a molecular biologist."

"Wow," was all I could muster so I could bite my tongue.

"Hi. I'm Gregory, Delia's boyfriend," he interjected. I was too busy with a joker's smile on my face staring at the shadow that hovered over my cousin's fiancé.

"Where is Nola? Sheila said she was your chaperone. You two aren't alone are you?"

"Nola is taking a nap at the hotel. Gregory knows his way around. He comes here every year." I held back the glare but gritted my teeth all the same.

"Oh, that's right honey, sorry about your psychotic mother. That's horrible that she left you at the age of five." My mother evidently had a nice long talk with Lisa and I was going to have a nice long scream at her later.

Gregory grabbed my hand and was pushing on the pressure point between my thumb and forefinger trying to calm me down. He knew I was on the verge of exploding. Not to mention the hovering image over Doug was coming closer as he extended his hand. I took it reluctantly, not sure what I was about to see or feel from him.

"You work privately finding protein identification tags for certain bacteria." I said as the stream of consciousness flowed through me.

"How did you know all that? I rarely get past the words molecular biologist before people's eyes glaze over. I don't even talk about my work with Kelly," he said in a light airy voice but his eyes bored though me. He wanted his work to remain secret and didn't like my little synopsis.

"You look the same Dee Dee," Kelly pretending to fix her dress around her huge boobs that popped out from her red sundress as she looked at my very small chest.

"Lactating already, when is this shotgun wedding?" I whispered under my breath just for her to hear.

Nola's word came back to me, *Lily and Gregory are both responsible for her death.* My words could pull someone from their path. I could become a Soul Shifter.

Gregory stopped me as they walked to sit in the sunroom around the covered pool. He put a finger to my lips. "Stop this and calm down right now."

I felt a little hazy and didn't appreciate it. I wanted to be sharp. I glared at him.

"What they say is inconsequential to me." Gregory said. "You need to be less obvious and pay attention to what you say. You'll upset Sheila if you have an outburst here. Now relax and control yourself."

"It's so unfair."

"You'll live." He pushed me forward to the wolves without a weapon in hand.

"Our Kelly is graduating from Stanford in May. Wasn't it nice of her to come and say hi during her spring break?"

"Imagine that. Well thanks a heap, Kell!" I was towing the line with Gregory who shot me a look.

I decided to excuse myself to meditate for five minutes in the bathroom because I still had to get through dinner. When I left the bathroom I had complete control over myself. I walked down the hall and saw a picture of my dad when he was young, his arm around Lisa.

"Feeling nostalgic?" Doug's voice echoed down the hall and made me jump. I noticed the shadow again.

"That's my Dad."

"I really don't like nosy people. Are you nosy Delia?" I really didn't understand what Kelly saw in him. Personally, he gave me the creeps.

"No, not by choice."

"Then, what are you?"

"I'm a high school student."

"I thought it was Kelly, but it's you. It's in the bloodline." His eyes stared deadly into mine.

*What?*

He grabbed my arm and when I was close I saw it. A flashing light shine from underneath his clothes. I was attracted to it and grabbed at it like a kitty playing with a flashlight. I felt him freeze. I saw splinters coming off this tear shaped light and I lightly placed them back in order then put the light back. He didn't seem to notice and continued to walk away. The light was brighter and didn't flash anymore. I sat down at the table and gave Gregory a small smile.

He looked at Doug suspiciously and with worry back at me. He mouthed, 'What happened?' I just shrugged with wide eyes. Truthfully I had no idea.

Doug seemed okay except he kept kissing Kelly with a huge smile on his face. Kelly jabbered on about her wedding in September and about how I was required as her only cousin, to be a bridesmaid. I chalked that one up to not having any friends. As we ate, I watched him closely. He never said a word or looked at me. Then Gregory asked Doug a question that started it all.

"So Doug, do you have a lab at a local university?"

"Oh, I don't believe in my work anymore. In fact, I'm planning on taking my Kelly on a vacation next week."

"Honey, what has gotten into you? I fly back on Friday to get ready for finals."

"There's no need for that. We should drink our way through Tuscany. Doesn't that sound nice?" Kelly gave him a sideways glance trying to stop him from being so embarrassingly ridiculous.

"Oh well, if you're not up for it, I'm going to have to say goodnight. I have to pack for my trip. I can't wait. I've always wanted to go. I continuously found myself in the lab trying to excel in my field and I have forgotten to enjoy life. Not anymore I'll tell you. Well, have a nice night." Kelly ran after him as he headed toward the door. Gregory took me aside.

"What did you do?"

"I'm not sure. I saw something gleaming from inside him. I grabbed it and put a group of tear-shaped crystals back together. It was a terrible mess. You should have heard his anger at me before I did that; now he's happy."

"Delia, that was his soul you reorganized. You can't do that; his soul thinks his life purpose is complete. He has no ambition now."

"I'm not sure. He isn't a nice person. I like him better this way, before he was so angry and bitter. Now he's looking forward to his vacation. Isn't that a good thing?"

"It was the frustration that would either help him complete his work or move on to something new. Either way he was productive. Now he thinks he is accomplished and is looking for Nirvana. He is not dead but he'll roam the earth until he is dead from irresponsibility. Life holds no importance for him now but he is searching for heaven and it isn't here, Delia. You have to fix it."

"Alright, I was just curious. I don't want him to die. Are you sure it felt right..."

"Yes. I'll distract Kelly while you make this right."

Doug was at his car and Kelly was standing in front of him as he tried to get in. She was in tears and I was feeling guilty. Gregory was able to guide her easily with the state she was in.

I let Doug get in his car as I jumped into the passenger side. I was sitting next to him and for some reason he didn't seem to see me. I wondered why he didn't speak to me but I didn't have time to think about it. I grabbed his light and he froze as before. I tried to pull it apart and it wouldn't budge. Then I thought of Candy and closed my eyes. I focused trying to crack it into shards being careful not to take any energy. It broke into shards the same way I found it. I placed it back inside him.

"Why am I in my car? What did you do?" The shadow was back looming over us.

"I'm not sure." I touched his cheek, trying to give him a little positive energy to balance all that anger but he slapped it away.

"Get out!"

"Goodbye, Doug. I hope you find what you're looking for."

Gregory masked Kelly's craziness and made it look like a misunderstanding. Whether he wanted to or not Doug was taking Kelly to Tuscany for their honeymoon. No one else heard Nirvana Doug because my Aunt and Uncle were busy in the kitchen at the time.

We went back to the hotel and I called my mom. I was too tired to yell at her about spreading the gossip on Gregory, but I made a mental note of it for when I got home. Nola let us sleep on the pullout in the next room together. It was the first time we were in a bed together and now I was in heaven. I woke up periodically and found him staring at me. He would kiss me then lull me back to sleep with a little haze. I could feel his hands on me and I wondered why he didn't want to play around. Nola was in the other room. She was asleep. I could hear her snoring.

*Didn't he want me?*

I dreamt of us enjoying each other many times. Now, this was real and I couldn't stay awake. The opportunity was gone. I decided in my dreams that night, to make it a priority to find out.

When we arrived at Oakwood Psychiatric Center, I had a sense of foreboding remembering the dream I had a few weeks back. I never told Gregory. He probably thought I didn't like hospitals because I was holding his hand so tightly.

The institution was very airy despite the heavy door that locked behind us. The windows along the one side from floor to ceiling overlooked a garden. We walked down the long hallway but unlike my dream, all the doors were open. Some of the residents were meandering the halls in different exaggerations of moods. They were either yelling or laughing continuously or had withdrawn blank stares that didn't acknowledge us as we walked by them.

Her room was empty when we entered it. Gregory and Nola didn't stop and turn to look for her, they circled the room looking at her things. I didn't understand at first. I thought it was a little weird that they were invading her privacy. Then I realized they were looking for signs that she was getting better. Gregory opened the closet door and on the inside were all these strange multidimensional pictures. He touched them slowly tracing the lines as if it were some Rosetta stone to her. He grabbed a couple and folded them neatly into his pocket. I went and stood next to him. His lips tightly presses together.

"They are mandalas. They use it as a type of art therapy here. It's the only communication she will give to anyone. She either stares into space or draws mandalas with only colored pencils. If you give her paint, crayons or markers she won't pick them up. Come on, Grandma, let's check the common room."

When we found her, she was drawing, facing a wall of windows. The whole common room was practically a greenhouse. If I went crazy I'm going to tell my mom to put me here. There were doors that led to exterior gardens so yes, you were confined, but if you were crazy, you didn't even know it.

"Hi mom, happy birthday." Gregory bent down and kissed her cheek. She kept drawing like he wasn't there.

He must have expected this because she had been deteriorating since he was seven, though it was still sad to watch him get rejected anyhow. One of the reasons Nola placed her here must have been to protect him and Lily from having to go through that every week or month. Once a year was probably the best for them that and it was a beautiful facility.

"This is my girlfriend, Delia. I wanted you to meet her. I love her very much." Gregory talked to her very matter of fact with no emotion. He pulled out the chair across from her and gestured for me to sit there.

"Hi. I like your mandalas. I've never seen drawings like these, but I'm not very artistic." I was babbling.

I figured looking stupid I could get away with her.

She continued to draw as I spoke then flipped the piece of paper over and slid it across the table, her hand remaining on top with fingers almost touching me. She was looking directly into my eyes. Her own eyes seemed cloudy and dull. I heard Nola gasp and Gregory grabbed her hand.

"Um, thank you."

I turned it over and looked at the colorful shapes inside a circle. I traced them with my index finger the same way Gregory had. Then I saw the shapes moving and floating into the air towards her head. My hands were getting hot and felt like they would burst. I held them up and looked at them. In my palms of my hands were the shapes in her mandala. She placed my hands on her head by grabbing at my wrists forcefully, like with Candy and then Gregory that one day our foreheads where touching. Gregory was pulling us apart and I heard both of us say in unison. "Please let us be!" I could feel my energy draining from my face, my heart then my belly. I knew I wasn't conscious anymore. My face still hurt when it hit the floor as two orderlies finally broke our connection.

*What was wrong with me? Why can't I have a normal day anymore?* I asked myself.

*"Because, you are not a normal girl, my Delia."* I heard my Great Aunt Helen answer before I awoke in the hospital.

"I think she's waking up." I heard my mom say in a far off voice. "Look her eyes keep opening then closing."

"Delia? Please wake up." Gregory was pushing himself into my mind with a light haze. My brain wanted to but my eyes wouldn't. "NOW! WAKE UP NOW." His voice reverberated into my head and vibrated what was left of my fried brain. I instantly opened my eyes and saw the back of my mother's head turned toward Gregory.

"Shush, Gregory. You don't have to yell at her. It won't help. Maybe you should go back-

"Delia!" His eyes widened and he pushed past my

mother in mid sentence. I groaned in response.

"Can you talk?" Why did Gregory look so tired?
I wondered.

"I'll go get someone." My mom said. When she left he
put his mouth down to my ear.

"TALK! TALK NOW!" He again pushed by yelling.
I felt my mouth open with another groan and drool come out.
*Lovely*, I'm a moron I thought. Tears appeared in his eyes now
as he wiped the drool with his sleeve.

"I'm so sorry, Delia. I didn't know she had any power
left." What was he talking, about I wondered. How long had
I been here? Where was here? I looked out the window and
saw palm trees. Florida still, okay I got one answer on my own.

The doctor came in with a smile on his face. He was
having a good day; one of his vegetables was awake.

"Well, hello Miss Stanton."

'Well, hello Doctor Morgan.' I wanted to say but more
drool came out with another groan. I could read his name tag.
He looked into my eyes with a small light.

"That's a good sign trying to talk. It shows ability to
produce motor functions." Thank you, I think. Literally.

"Can you move your toes?" I tried to feel them and felt
my feet flop slightly.

"Good and your fingers?" I lifted my hand with
no problem.

"Now Delia, I know you don't know why you're here.
When the paramedics took your temperature it was a hundred
and five, which made you have a grand mal seizure. Then you
lapsed into a coma for ten days. What caused the fever, we're
not sure, maybe a virus, but you'll be just fine with some rehab.
You can even be transferred in a couple days to
Cleveland Clinic."

My mom followed the doctor outside to talk alone
about my recovery. Gregory stayed but stood across the room,
his face looked like it was going to fall off.

He was blaming himself for everything.

"Don pwaise?" came out. It was supposed to be, 'Don't please?' As in don't blame yourself…don't hurt. I tried to talk to Gregory. My tongue lied dead inside my mouth.

His eyes welled up with tears as he ran to my side, held my hand and then collapsed to his knees next to my bed. I felt his guilt and sadness start to flow through me.
He looked up at me and quickly dropped my hand.

"Lay may" I wanted to say 'Let me'. *Let me take the pain away.*

"No, you need to take care of you right now. Delia, you are trying to heal my pain. You are in a hospital bed because of me. I hurt everyone I love." I had sudden fear he might leave and never come back. I wouldn't be able to stop him.

'Please,' I prayed, 'Help me be able to talk so I can ease his pain. I need him here with me. He is my air.'

A male nurse stepped in and injected something into my IV and took my pulse then left. Afterward, just like that, the words found my tongue and I could move my lips more easily.

"Stop it. I'll be fine. As long as we are together everything will work out. I'm nothing without you. My soul was only functioning when I met you. Now I'm living. I would rather live one more day with you, then a hundred years alone. It is my path and I choose this life with you, unless…you don't love me anymore."

"Now you stop it. Loving you is like touching the stars, it is what I was made for, why I'm here," he said.

I could tell I was reaching him and my fears were eased. I would walk off a cliff if he asked me to and not because of his ability. If I died because of him it would be worth it, I thought, *He is worth it all.*

# CHAPTER 10

When I woke up the next morning, the same male nurse was staring at me at the end of my bed. He seemed upset about something and my brain was still too fried to care but 'stupid me' grabbed his hand when he was replacing the bag for my IV. In a green haze I saw a young girl a couple floors down sick with...

"Leukemia...your sister has Leukemia."
I said out loud accidentally.

"How do you know that? Not even my best friend that works here knows that. We have different last names and I have made it a point not to let on who I am, otherwise they won't let me take care of her on the night shift."

"You work a night shift, too?"

"Please don't change the subject. How do you know about my sister?"

"I sort of see things sometimes."

"You're psychic. Really?"

"You don't seem surprised."

"I have read a lot about psychics. I just never thought I would meet one that was really truly one. There are so many fakes out there."

"Well I don't charge for my service or anything." I was joking, but he didn't seem to notice.

"Did you see anything else? Will we find a bone marrow match?"

"No, I only saw the present. You're not her so it's kind of secondary information. I'm only allowed to see how it's affecting you not her. Aren't siblings always a match?"

"No, not always. You see, I'm only her half brother. That is why we have different last names; my mother remarried when I was three."

"I'm sorry. I wish I could help."

"Do you think you might be willing to go down to her room in a wheel chair and see if you get anything? I normally don't ask this of people, but you're kind of special and I have special circumstances. I won't be able to go with you because I can't risk leaving my floor during my shift or being up there in the day time."

"Is it alright for me to move around?"

"Doctor's orders were to get the patient out of bed for therapy. Afterward if you're up to it, you could drop in to see her."

"Um…alright. I'll try." Just then Gregory walked in.

"Hi. This is my boyfriend, Gregory." My face flushed. "This is my nurse… oh um I'm sorry I don't know your name." I searched for a name tag.

"Oh yes, I'm Luke." He shook hands with me and gave a wave to Gregory. Gregory kind of scrunched his face looking confused.

"I will send an aid in to get you ready for therapy. Remember, Room 220b, Theresa Hernandez, if you get a chance."

"Sounds good." I smiled.

Gregory stood there gawking at me until I asked, "What's wrong?"

"You've decided to speak English again."

"Huh?"

"You were speaking Spanish I think it was, with that nurse."

"I don't know Spanish. I have enough trouble with the

English language."

"Well unless I'm having an aneurism, I couldn't understand a word you two were saying."

"Hey, wait a second. When I first woke up I was having trouble speaking. I was so worried about you so I prayed for a way to talk to you. Then he appeared and I was able to create full sentences when before I couldn't say one word. His last name is Cantilano; he is Latino so he must speak Spanish. It was *him*. He has an ability to help others speak."

"Huh…well I was beginning to feel left out."

"I'm sorry. It was completely innocent."
I rolled my eyes.

"I know. You're my girl." He smiled at me.

"Yes, I am." I smiled back and then beckoned him closer for a kiss.

Therapy was harsh. I was able to walk, but my balance was terrible. I couldn't stand for longer than ten seconds without needing assistance. The assessment was good enough that I could go home but I would need some sort of outpatient services when I went back to Cleveland in a couple of days. I was happy that I could sleep in my own bed soon. After we were finished, I wheeled myself to Room 220b in Pediatrics. A very skinny girl about my age looked up from her book and smiled. Her skin was grayish and her lips her almost blue.

"You must be Delia. My brother called me and told me you might drop by. He said you have the sight. I love psychic phenomena. This bubbly little girl is my cousin Zoe." She was to the left and I barely noticed her.
I was stunned by Theresa's appearance.

"Hey, who is going to win the World Series?" Zoe asked in a squeaky voice.

"Um, my gift doesn't work that way. It helps sometimes if I can touch something or someone."

"Zoe, hush. You'll have to excuse her, she can get a little hyper. Thank you for coming."

"Well I'm not sure what I can do but I'll try."

"I'll be happy with anything you can come up with."

I wasn't too sure about that. What if I saw something that wasn't good? I was starting to think that this might be a very bad idea. She was studying me and tilted her head like she heard my thoughts.

"It's okay, Delia," She said in a very wise voice. "I know the possibilities. This is really for Luke so he knows he did everything he could. He is so overworked looking after me here, working double shifts to pay my medical expenses. If you see that I am going to die then maybe he will accept it as I have had to. You see, I've been told I have months left. I think it is more like weeks. So you won't be telling me anything that I don't already know." She sat up and moved her legs over the side of the bed. I could see bruises on her legs that went all the way up to the edge of her gown.

"Please," she asked and stretched her arms out with palms up. My hands started to shake. I wanted to help so badly I wanted to give her life. I wanted to do more than just see her death. I wanted to find her a solution.

*Please* I prayed, *Give me something to help her.*

I found my courage in my head. The warmth came from my heart and ran all the way down to my palms.

*Thank you.* I didn't feel alone in this pursuit any longer.

I could feel a presence there in the air. I let my hands hover over hers, closed my eyes and then braced for what was to come when our hands touch. I could feel the energy flowing from my heart into her but I saw nothing. The heat in the room temperature was at least ninety or maybe it was me. Then I felt my body convulsing and I was on the floor. I smiled up at Theresa as she screamed for a nurse. I heard Zoe say, "Theresa your bruises are gone. That was so cool!" Then I blacked out.

My eyes didn't focus right away and the room was spinning as I opened them. Gregory was there at the end of my bed looking pissed.

"How long?" I asked.

"Two hours. Are you trying to kill yourself?" His eyes were guarded and I could tell he wanted to scream at me.

"How is Theresa? I saw her legs, her bruises were gone."

"You can't just give your energy away without making sure you are healed yourself first. They think you have epilepsy." He pointed out the door at the nurse's station. "Your mother is worried sick."

"I'm a healer, Gregory. I helped her. Just think of how many others there are that I could help."

"Listen to me right now." He was pushing my mind. "You are not to heal anyone else until you yourself are better."

"Stop trying to control me. Besides, it won't work. I am in a better mindset than you are right now."

"You are not a superhero, Delia. Helping Theresa almost put you in a coma again. Healing my mother," his mouth curled in disgusted, "almost killed you."

"Your mother? She's better?"

"That's not the point! You are harming yourself by healing."

"You knew and didn't tell me. That's why Nola's not here. You didn't want me to know that I was a healer. That I helped your mother." I spat a little with the last word.

"I was going to tell you after you were finished with therapy here. I need you alive and my mother almost killed you for the sake of her own sanity."

"It's not her fault, Gregory. Have you talked with her?"

"No. She almost killed the woman I love. I hate her."

"Don't say that! I want you to go see her now."

"No."

"I'm not talking to you until you do. Plus I'm angry that you weren't forthcoming about my new ability."

"Well obviously I was right. You go off healing the first patient you come across here and almost end up in another coma." He was pacing and crazily waving his arms.

"You have no faith, Gregory Carlisle."

"Not when it comes to you. You were meant for me.
There is no one in this world that could ever replace you.
I won't let you destroy yourself. That is why I'm here to guide
you and love you. Oh yeah, I guess now to keep you alive."

"Calm down Gregory. It will be all right. I'm all right."

"Why were you in that girl's room in the first place?"
He stood there with his arms crossed slightly glaring at me.

"I was asked by one of her family members to see if
I could find a bone marrow donor for her if there was one.
I really wanted to help but her situation was obviously grim.
I asked for guidance so that I could do something to give some
possible hope. Then suddenly I was healing her."

"How did you have time to talk to anyone? You were
here with that male nurse, and then you were in therapy."
I didn't say anything as he deliberated. I really didn't want him
going after Luke. Things could get ugly. I heard him mumble,
"Spanish Speaking Silver Tongue."

All I could do was sigh because Gregory was tiring
me out. I wouldn't be able to stop him from being the
overprotective boyfriend. I could see the future without even
touching him. Any minute Luke was going to come in to thank
me and Gregory was going to throw him up against the wall.

"Hey, could you go get me a Coke? The machine is
out on this floor. You have to go to the first." I made my voice
sound hoarse.

"Are you trying to sidetrack me?"

"No, I'm just really thirsty for something other
than water."

"Okay, but we are going to finish this when
I come back."

"Fine," I said as he stomped out of the room hoping he
would calm down before he returned.

About a minute later there was Luke's smiling face. He
was trying to get new tests for his sister ordered by her doctor

to determine what had happened. He had snuck down to see her after they brought me up unconscious. She wasn't pale or bruised anymore. It was obvious something had changed in her condition. I couldn't tell him for sure but I knew whatever had happened it was something positive. Maybe I was able to at least buy her some time. This healing thing was new to me and I really didn't know to what extent I was able to make it work.

I told Luke as much and then told him to wait a while before he came back to my room. When Gregory did come back, he slammed my Coke down on my tray table. As I looked up, startled, about to ask, 'What?' He turned the screen on and there was a picture of a hospital on the local news.

"What's wrong?"

He pointed back up to the screen and there was Luke and Theresa's cousin talking. Standing next to Zoe was a woman in her thirties I guessed was her mother.

"Oh no," was all I could say as she talked about some patient named Delia that healed her cousins bruises and maybe cured her Leukemia for good.

"Oh yes, we have to get you out of here as soon as possible."

"Zoe is young. She doesn't understand. She probably thought I'd like the attention." All I could do was shrug.

"This is very dangerous for you, especially when her tests come back clean. That little girl has just turned you into a possible media frenzy." He was grabbing my stuff shoving it into a duffle bag. "We have to get you discharged."

"My mother won't consent to that. Not to mention that she has no idea about what I am now."

"What you are is Delia and who you are has always been there. I think she loves you more now than she ever has since you have learned all this about yourself. We'll just show her a little glimpse, not the whole picture. Let her accept it one step at a time. We'll tell her that you touched this girl and she became well. Now we have to leave. You are a target for the media. We don't have to tell the whole story right away."

"You mean like you did with me." I said glaring at him.

He just raised an eyebrow. Obviously I had caught on to his little plan of How to Guide Delia 101.

"Okay. I'll trust your judgment, but I'm still scared. I don't want her to hate me. She always looked at me like I was an alien when I did things like this as a kid."

"She can't hate you. Just because you have different thoughts and feelings than hers, is not a good enough reason. They are what make you...well, you. I'll go and get her for you." Gregory found her talking to the doctor still about my latest seizure.

"Oh good, honey, you're up. We were just going over different medications that might help this little problem of yours." Mom was trying to fix her broken Delia - what a surprise.

"Mom, I don't have epilepsy."

"Really. Well we're here to find out."

"I have to go Mom."

"No, honey. We can't leave. We don't even have the results to your scans yet. The doctor is looking at them now."

"I want to go home. We have to, right now."

"Why? Why do you want to leave today?"

"I have this thing happening to me. I was talking to this girl downstairs and I held her hand. You see, she has Leukemia and is, or was, going to die."

"Oh that is just too bad for her. Maybe you should stay away from her. That kind of thing could affect your recovery." Gregory put his hands on her shoulders.

"You must listen to her, Sheila." I could see him concentrating.

"What is going on you two?"

"Mom, when I touched her I had a seizure and now she's better. Her family and well now the media think I healed her. The sick girl has a cousin who talked to the local news.

They are now doing tests to confirm it today. I want to go home." I said it all very slowly and softly, trying to reach her. She was finally absorbing it.

"We should leave right now Sheila." Gregory put a hand on her shoulder. "Go talk to her doctor and have her discharged." Gregory helped me try to get her to understand.

"Okay," was all she said as she blindly turned and left. I felt the crushing blow of fear.

"I'm not sure if she accepts the situation or if that was just your influence on her. She definitely wasn't happy." I said to Gregory sadly.

"It will be alright. Remember, she can't hate you. You were honest and that is all people ask of each other. I want you to understand, how she feels is not your fault or your responsibility. She will deal with it and then come around."

"I hope you're right." My mom was back and pale-faced.

"I guess the doctor was already aware of the situation. He has agreed that it would be best for you and the hospital if you leave. You're stable and the hospital can't afford the publicity either way if that girl turns out to be better or not. I guess it is too much of a risk with their finicky contributors. Someone will be by with discharge papers soon." She said nothing more and I was crushed.

She rushed around as if busy, never looking at me. Had I disappointed her by not being normal? All I knew for sure was that in her eyes, from now on, I was an alien.

# CHAPTER 11

The ride home was quiet, but my insides turned with the emotions that wafted from my mother. I feared she would never understand. Can the love a mother has for her child transcend her belief system? Could she love me when I was considered to be a Mentalist? All I could think was 'I'm sorry I'm not what you wanted. Maybe one day I can make you proud of me despite this condition.'

Gregory sat next to me every once in awhile giving my leg a pat or my hand a light squeeze telling me it was going to be okay. I wasn't convinced. I saw a flock of birds flying by and a childhood memory flash back that was long buried.

I was ten and at a fancy restaurant on the lake with my parents. It was my mom's birthday and a few weeks before we found out my dad was sick. I pointed at the floor to ceiling windows and said, "A seagull is going to hit the window right by your head, Dad."

He asked, "Oh, really? And what does that mean, my little sage?"

I followed with, "It means that he wants you to see a doctor. Either way, your fate will be the same as his, sooner or later."

Then a seagull slammed itself against the window breaking its neck, leaving a bloody streak on the window right above my dad's head. My mother stared at me with the fear of a frightened child. She begged him not to go to the doctor. He knew I was gifted in some paranormal way. I told him when his mother, my grandmother, had passed away before she was found dead from a heart attack. He knew that I was gifted in some way.

My mother always acted as if I had cursed him that day. What she didn't know was that I myself had no idea what the warning meant till a year after he died. I didn't understand the word fate. I wasn't allowed.

I lingered, resisting the pull of the universe from every direction as it placed obstacles trying to put me on this path. The path that my mother didn't want me to ever follow, with certain abilities she considered to have killed her husband. My gift to the world was the curse she hated and it was a part of me now. I breathed psychic energy, and the more and more I practiced, the more I liked myself for who I was.

We dropped Gregory off and I almost expected her to tell me to get out there with him. She politely said goodnight to him while I clung to him through the shuttle's open window. He kissed me and told me he would be at my house tomorrow morning so my mom could go back to work. I didn't even start with him about school. He wouldn't hear of it.

*Later,* I thought, *I will make my point later. Now I had to deal with my mother's silent treatment.*

She helped me to bed without a word. She left my room with her back turned. I thought I heard her say, "Goodnight", but I think that I imagined it.

My dreams flooded in my head quickly, probably from the medication I was still on. My dad was smiling at me and we were standing in a field of violets. There was an eagle that circled above that every once in a while gave me its point of view, letting me see myself out of my body as it flowed though the air. I was the eagle then I was 'me' and I realized I could switch back and forth as I wished. He laughed at my fascination, although I couldn't hear him. He pointed up and mouthed the words 'go for it'. With that, I was flying over mountains and forests until I saw buildings that appeared in the city. I saw the date and time flashing on a bank's moving digital sign that read July 7th 4:21 pm. That was when I noticed the white fog cascading around what I was seeing now; this was the future.

I caught a glimpse of myself walking towards one of the very tall buildings and there were six others following behind. I quickly flew onto the future 'me's' shoulder that didn't flinch or smack me away but I/she let me sit there. For some reason I could recognize me, but not the others whose faces where obscured by blurriness of the vision. We stood in a 'V' formation, linking hand in hand, and a warm glow came from my body as I was speaking. I really wished I could read lips; I tried. I found myself back in the field with not only my dad now but Lily also. She reached up and touched my cheek then so did my dad. Sounds of white noise filled the air. I was barely able to hear them as they spoke.

The two of them shouted in unison, "You have been shown, do more than just see. Things are as they are, you must live through what has to be."

Then Lily alone said, "Find the five golden rings."

And Dad said, "Seven isn't enough. There must be nine. The music will lead you to the fork."

I awoke with a start. So many riddles, at least I knew the date and time now. My mother's opinion couldn't matter if I was to fulfill the prophecy. Maybe dad could send her a dream, too. She wouldn't think it was real, anyway.

I couldn't wait for her to understand. I didn't have time. While my mom was helping me with my shower the next morning, I kept trying to read her thoughts through her emotions, which as I was coming to realize was quite dangerous. A person can be anxious about many things good or bad. I felt waves of continuous fear and I wasn't sure if it was a fear for me or of me. I realized the irony, as I sat in the tub, cold and naked waiting for her to get me a towel.

Her judgment meant everything right now, though it wasn't supposed to. I was told to let go, how the hell was I supposed to do that? Will she still love me if she hated who I was? She didn't raise me to be this way; it was instinctual, built into me before I was conceived. I watched her walk back and forth as she helped me dress and she still said nothing, her face solemn and serious never making eye contact.

"Mom?" I reached for her as she pulled up my jeans.

"Not right now, Delia," she said in an almost whisper.

"When then?"

"I need time to process all of this." This meaning me, she had no idea what to do with me. She didn't even know the whole story yet, and I wondered what would happen when she did. Then I thought she never would, she wouldn't know the real me because she didn't want to.

"I have to know, do you still love me?"

"Of course I do." I saw her profile as she searched for a pair of socks in my drawer, her eyes looked up. She seemed to anticipate my next question as if praying I won't ask it.

"Are you afraid of me?" She turned around and looked me directly in the eyes.

"I have always been afraid of these abnormal activities." And with that, she left the room leaving me there alone. I sat there listening to her put away the dishes. When Gregory was at the door, she told him where to go for therapy with the last words, "Tell Delia goodbye for me."

That is when I lost it. The tears spewed out and I fell back from my sitting position onto my bed looking up at the swirls on the ceiling as the wetness fell on my just blown dry hair. I tried to pull my legs up into a fetal position. They wouldn't cooperate and were too heavy. Frustrated, I rolled on my side, feeling broken in more ways than one. Then he was there behind me, his arms wrapping around mine.

"There is no pain." He whispered. "There is only

knowledge and acceptance. Hear me now Delia. I won't let this hurt you. It isn't fair what you have to deal with, that you feel this kind of pain. So I order you not to feel it. You will feel only my love in your heart."

He rolled my face forward and kissed me so lightly that it made a confusion erupt. The pain I was experiencing was being replaced by every kiss with his love and my sadness turned to longing. I wanted more than just kisses. This time I didn't want him to stop.

Staring at his face, I slowly glided my hand down his chest to his belly until I found the button at the top of his jeans. He was there already with his opposite hand interlocking our fingers blocking the attempt. So I used the other hand this time placing my hand on his thigh and then moved up holding his hip then going for the button again. He parried by pulling both of my hands above my head nuzzling my nose. He continued to make love to me with my clothes on, kissing my neck and ears.

"Be with me," I pleaded.

"Always," he said and continued kissing me. He knew what I meant; he was just trying to let me down nicely.

"Please Gregory," I traced my lips lightly along his cheekbone feeling the soft hairs as they led to whiskers.

"Not now, not today." He spoke softly.

"But why?"

He sighed, "You're not ready, trust me. I wasn't ready and I'm a guy. Let's just enjoy this part and move forward when you're a little older."

"We are the same age. I want you. Isn't that enough to be ready?" I didn't understand.

*Weren't guys obsessed with sex? Why didn't he want to tear my clothes off?*

"No, there needs to be a level of commitment. That is what I took from my first time. It has to be more than just wanting."

"But I love you, Gregory, and I will always love you."

"There is the love we feel and show then there is the love we share."

"Not only are you losing me. You're killing the mood."

"You and I need to grow together, learn and sometimes sacrifice before we are ready have sex or make love. We must strengthen our bond as a couple giving and taking, communicating."

"You mean like right now." I grimaced and rolled my eyes. All this talking was really boring me. I wanted to not think…I needed to act on impulse. Obviously, I wasn't going to be getting any for a very long time. He was too sensible. Damn it! He saw I wasn't taking him seriously and he was getting annoyed.

"Listen Delia, if we have sex before you're ready, you will resent me, and I am not going to let that happen."

*Today I was rejected by my mother, couldn't he give me this one thing? Didn't he love me enough to fulfill this one desire?* My rejection was turning to anger.

"My mom doesn't want me, you don't want me-

"Don't you dare," He angrily pointed his finger. "Do you think having the level head in this relationship is easy? I daydream hourly about putting my hands and lips all over your body. Thinking about what your face will look like at the first instance we are one." I gasped in shock.

The idea of him fantasizing about me was flattering. He was trying to be a gentleman. Well a gentleman with naughty thoughts. I smiled as I thought about us as 'one'.

"I'm sorry. I didn't realize that you wanted me, too. Sometimes it seems that I'm some sort of obligation. You never seem to need me the way I need you. I have often wondered if I am attractive or sexy to you at all."

"You have no idea how often you stir me up to the point I might go completely ballistic." As I sat up on the bed, my legs slightly dangling over the edge, he stood up then kneeled before me.

"Wow! I knew you loved me, but knowing you feel that way…" I was at a loss of words.

"Delia, can't you feel it, I mean, doesn't your empathic ability show you how crazy you make me?" He placed his hands on my cheeks his face directly in mine.

"I guess it kind of all meshes together, my emotion and yours when we make out. It's like I don't know where I end and you begin."

"Well, now you know. Maybe you could tone it down a little until we are ready to take that next step." His use of we was ridiculous. These were strictly his lame-o rules.

"I'll try if we can negotiate the terms." I threw it back at him just for fun.

"Well see. Now, we have got to get you to therapy."

"We could always blow it off." I began wrapping my arms around him with a sly smile.

"Delia you just said you'd try." Ending our witty we banter with his irritated tone.

"Fine," I said with a shrug.

I knew his crazy reasoning and I understood. It wasn't a rejection. It was some absurd noble sacrifice. Way to save the day, Gregory. Any normal teenager girl could throw herself into meaningless sex to forget her parental rejection. I had to get the boyfriend with morals. Fun!

"That was amazing!" Gregory exclaimed.

"Well I'm glad you enjoyed it because I found it quite painful." I said with great disgust.

"Oh come on, it wasn't THAT bad and with a little practice, I'm sure it will become much easier."

"I know for sure that I will never get used to all those jerky movements. I hated every minute of it."

"They were only jerky because you need to get your strength back; you'll get the groove."

"Why don't you just date him, you're so into taking his side!"

"I'm sorry. If getting you to walk across a room means being on the physical therapists side, then I'm all for a mutiny. Delia, in one short hour with those leg exercises you're already moving better. In a few weeks, you'll be back to your old self."

"Keep it up and I'm going to buy you a set of pom poms."

"Sure, I'm game. I'm going to be focusing all my energy on getting you well."

"You can't do that! You have school and graduation."

"No, I don't anymore. I'm getting my GED. I already talked it over with Grandma."

"That's nice. When are you going to start talking to me about these things? Don't I count?"

"That is exactly why I'm doing this. You mean so much. I can't do it all, go to school and look after you. It's May and I have finals in three weeks. I can't catch up even if I wanted to. I'm going to get back with my tutor and get my GED."

"What about when I go back to school and work?"

"Then I'll have more time to study."

"Wait. Where are we going?"

"I'm taking you home to have lunch."

"No take me to your house. I want to see Nola."

"Yeah…not today."

"Why not? I miss her."

"Because I think you could use a nap. You look tired."

"Yes and I can nap on the couch like I always do. What is going on?"

"My mom is here."

"Here? You mean in Cleveland?"

"Yes, she got back a few days ago."

"Wow!"

"Yeah, I know."

"She hasn't been home in-"Twelve years."

"Have you talked with her?"

"No, and I'm not going to. Neither are you."

"Come on there isn't any more danger. You're being a little overbearing."

"Forget it."

"Listen, I love you but you're acting like you are the boss of me and guess what? You're not!"

"You weren't there for ten days watching you motionless and pale, being fed threw tubes. Not knowing when or if you were going to wake up."

"How can someone who puts so much stock in fate have so little faith?"

"Things never work out like they've been planned. Even if it is a prophecy we still have free will."

"Is this about your sister?"

"Lily was supposed to be here. She was part of the Alignment and then she gets pregnant and dies in a car accident. So now everything has shifted. I don't know what's around the corner anymore."

"Oh, I think I can guarantee you that everything is falling into place."

"Really? And how can you do that?"

"I had a dream last night that gave me somewhat of an idea."

"You've been holding back on me?"

"You're not the only one who can have secrets."

"What?" He scowled.

"Nola and you have always kept me in the dark trying to protect me and that's got to stop. Last night I found out the date and this prophecy is about to be revealed very soon but before I tell you what I know, we have to get something straight. I'm the leader and you two are going to need to be more forthcoming from now on. I mean, I want to know everything at the same time as you two do. Got it?"

"When?"

"No, not till you both promise."

"Fine." He growled as he backed the car out of my driveway heading towards his house.

Walking through the door to the Cross House was nerve racking. Not for me, but for Gregory, which I have never experienced from him. I was worried about his mixture of fear and anger towards his mother and I had no idea what reaction was going to surface. He helped me to sit down in a chair in the foyer. He kneeled in front of me taking my hand. He was trying to appeal to my sensitive nature to get what he wanted.

"Will you sit here for a minute? I need to ask her a question alone. Do you mind?" He batted those bright green eyes, stopping my heart for a second.

"Of course not. I have the magazine I borrowed from the therapy office. I'll chill out here a bit. Take as much time as you need."

"Thanks." His smile was one of victory.

"Oh, but Gregory? I will be talking with her today. Got it?"

"Sure thing, sweets." He said as he quickly ran into the other room.

After reading an article on some singer I didn't know and her new love interest being the director in the movie she was staring in, I heard a car pull up the drive. I turned and stood up to look out the side window to see a man walking back and forth curiously, from his Vapor to the house's front stoop. Then I saw him looking up to the sky gesturing angrily. I was getting that feeling again like the first day I met Gregory. There was an urgency to open the door and let this apparent crazy person in the house.

*Oh what the hell*, I thought. I have trusted my instincts this far. I might as well surrender at this point.

"Can I help you?" I called out the front door.

"Hi. Is Nola here?" His intense stare was not hard to recognize.

"Uh yes…" I couldn't say another word as he walked past me into the house.

*Crap, Gregory was going to flip.*

"Don't you even have a smile for your dad, Lily?" By the way he was looking at me, I'd swear he knew I wasn't his daughter.

"Um…I'm not-

"What the hell are you doing here?" Gregory's voice boomed from behind me it was so harsh, I jumped a little.

"Listen Greg, you're never going to get very far with a greeting like that. Didn't Nola teach you any manners? Here I'll go first. Hello son, how are you doing?"

"I don't know. Ask my therapist about my abandonment issues."

"You're just upset that I haven't given you your present yet."

"I don't want anything from you. Get out!" Gregory didn't even see that he was being sarcastic.

*Why was he trying to get Gregory nuts?*

"Lily please explain to your brother-

"She is not Lily! Lily is dead!"

"Really huh? When did this happen?"

"Last August Phin." An unfamiliar voice came from behind.

"Is this true Miranda? Is our Lily really gone?" They were caring words with a cool demeanor.

"Where have you been Phineas? All this time our children needed you."

"I did exactly as you requested that day so long ago. I had a prosperous life."

"Why don't you go back to it because we don't need you." Gregory's face reddened.

"I can't. I was invited."

"No one in this house would want to see you come back!" Gregory growled.

"I was drawn here by plaguing dreams and visions until I drove my Vapor here from San Diego."

"He is telling the truth, Gregory." I went to hold his hand but it was clenched.

"Yes, it would appear that your family's prophecy is coming to pass." Phin smiled.

"How are you apart of this?" Gregory glared.

"Why Greg, I am a child of the Alignment also. Didn't Nola ever tell you?" Phin's eyes were innocent though his mouth smirked with mischief.

"So was Lily, but things change!" Gregory voice got louder.

"Oh come on, Greg. My dad wasn't in the picture for me either and I'm not crying tears into my paddle pool." Phin gestured a finger wiping a pretend tear from his face.

That was it. Gregory swung his readied punch hitting Phin so hard that he fell back rubbing his jaw. Recovering, Phin righted his posture with a strange smile across his face. Meanwhile, he was looking at me the whole time.

# CHAPTER 12

Gregory stormed upstairs to his room. Suddenly, I felt the need to get some fresh air and excused myself knowing Nola, Miranda and Phin wanted to talk. I really wasn't very comfortable being there, but I didn't want to leave Gregory either.

I slowly walked and limped my way to the back sliding door trying to be inconspicuous, as the three of them went at each other.

It was nice being out there on the patio. I hadn't gotten the chance to say hi to spring. I was in shock how quickly everything was growing. When we left for Florida, everything was still hibernating. Now, the vibrant colors energized me and for the first time in three days, I let my mind wander thinking of the dream I had last night and of how happy my dad seemed in it.

*I was going to recover and finish this prophecy business,* I thought with hope in my heart.

I heard the sliding door behind me and I was enjoying myself too much to turn around.

"You must be Delia." Phin's voice boomed from behind me.

*Here we go,* I thought, *I guess I'm next on Phin's list to annoy.*

"Yes, I am." I turned and looked at him thinking that Gregory was only going to get sexier with age. Then the thought of Gregory and I in bed together popped in my head, making me smile a little. "Boy do you know how to make an entrance."

"I always do. How long have you and my son been together?" There was something about the way he said been together that made my insides squirm. I suddenly felt naked and crossed my arms protecting myself.

"How's the jaw Phin?" My defenses told me when in doubt, answer a question with a question.

"Not so bad, but I could use some medical attention. Do you want to play nurse, Delia?" I wanted to scream, 'You creep! You can't be that stupid!' Then I realized what he was doing. He was trying to make it appear like he was hitting on me. There was no sensation that he was sexually attracted. Just a cold stonewall. He knew when I told the rest of them we could make the decision to kick him out of our little party. He couldn't leave, and wow, did he want to.

If I rejected him from the group maybe he could. Until then, he was being held by some unknown compulsion to be here and it was that same force that brought him here in the first place.

"You should use your gifts for good not evil."

"You really are the leader. A spunky little teenager with…ah, yes, daddy issues too. No wonder Gregory and you bonded so quickly."

I looked up, deflecting his sexual stare knowing now where Gregory got it from. With Phin, it was manipulative, almost cruel. Gregory was never cruel and he never used his ability to control others in a harmful way.

"Just because you saw my Dad in those the pictures inside your head doesn't mean I have daddy issues." A surprised look appeared on his face then I felt fear flood from him.

"He left you." Man, he was brutal.

"He died." I said lightly.

"He still abandoned you in some fashion and…oh you're mother doesn't understand you. How quaint and very boring." He puffed his lips out like he was talking to a baby. I was feeling the urge to hit him, too. Nola mentioned once that Gregory and Lily's father was an intellectual snob. I was starting to get what she meant.

"You have no idea what you're messing with, old man."

Old was extreme; he was more 'seasoned mature', with smoldering eyes. Just looking at him was exciting.

Then I asked, "Why don't you want to be here?"

He raised his right eyebrow the same way Gregory did when he was found out. Like that was such an unusual occurrence for someone to see through his little act probably because most women couldn't get past their hormones. My guess was that getting laid was not this guy's problem.

"I have my reasons, one mainly being that I am selfish and have other things to do besides change this world." One thing I've learned is that people who say that they're selfish usually aren't. This gave me some hope.

"Ah, so you believe it."

"Nola might not be the most powerful but her family's line is strong and should be respected. They can be traced back to the Druids," he said in a bored voice, while he stared at his manicured nails.

"And yet you still want me to release you from your obligation here? Something that has been around for thousands of years, to give this world a new start."

"Yes." He said with a sigh, "I can't believe I need the permission of a child to leave the city."

"You were sent here for a reason. I can't just discount that… no, I think we should give this a week at least." The power was so intoxicating it made me smile. Phin swiftly grabbed my shoulders and put his face an inch from mine.

"You stupid girl. You have no idea what you're playing with. Can't you see this is hurting them, that I am hurting them being here?" He growled threw his teeth, spitting in my face slightly. His cool demeanor was gone. I was pleased to be finally getting into the nitty-gritty. Phin's real motives for wanting to leave were being revealed. Squinting my eyes, I mulled over his reaction and a red haze rolled in.

Gregory's mother was sitting on the floor rocking back and forth. Two kids encircled her yelling and screaming as the front door to a very nice colonial opened and closed. As soon as Phin saw her, he ran toward her and pulled her up by her arms. "Miranda what's wrong, did you have another vision?"

"No. I felt your emotions this morning when you left and it has been tearing me up. I think I am becoming an empath."

"No, that can't be! You'll go insane with the intensity of your visions."

"You don't love me the way I love you." She said in a spacey voice. "You feel trapped here and want to leave."

"No!"

"You have been lying to me about the passion you feel and have been using you ability to convince me that you want me, when really you resent me and our family."

"Please, Miranda!"

"You know how I feel about love, Phineas. You are my best friend, but I refuse to be seen as an obstacle and our children shouldn't be seen as anything other than blessings."

"I won't ever leave you."

"What about when Lily comes becomes an empath herself. She'll know how you really feel about her. How will she ever be able to see herself as anything, but unwanted? I won't have that! Do you hear me?"

"I do love you all, I just feel that we got married too young. We were nineteen and crazy. I will see this through."

"The hell you will. I don't want my children to know the truth that you see them as obligations. When you're ready to love us the way we deserve, come back, otherwise have a prosperous life Phin. I release you, now I want you to go."

Phin turned without hesitation and left through the door he just came through. The worst part was the sound of a four-year old Gregory yelling Daddy from the front room window.

"GET YOUR HANDS OFF HER!" Gregory came from nowhere pushing his father to the ground, ending the vision. "You don't touch her. Do you understand me?"

"Did you see it Delia? Did you see their pain? What I put them through." Phin said looking up at me.

"It's okay Gregory." I said. "I was just talking to your dad and he misunderstood me."

"You're going to let me leave?" Phin asked.

"I don't know how," I shrugged. "If you're going to upset Gregory this much, maybe I should find out. Before he kills you."

"Yeah, let's find a way to get him out of here." Gregory spat. "We don't need him!"

Gregory sounded like a child. Usually he was the one telling me to go meditate. My world was turning upside down and in this weird reality this Gregory was irrational. Of course, in the old reality, Gregory didn't have parents. Today, he had his mother and father thrown at him all at once.

"It's okay, baby." I tried to absorb his anger like before. He kept building on it, creating more with every breath.

"No, it's not. You left us! And now you're a part of the Alignment? It could be months before it comes to pass. I can't stand looking at you for even a minute. You-make-me-sick!" Gregory's last sentence was delivered through clenched teeth.

Then Phin did something strange when Gregory turned to leave, dragging me with him. He grabbed Gregory and tackled him to the ground holding him in a headlock that seemed impossible to get out of no matter how much he struggled. He wasn't hurting him, but detaining. I clung to the brick wall surrounding the raised garden trying to regain my balance.

"Let me go, you son of a bitch! You could have hurt her!" Gregory yelled at the top of his lungs.

"Now I'm going to assume that you normally have better manners than this especially in front of a lady. I can only guess that I'm the major catalyst for such a horrible display." *This is from the guy who just asked me to play nurse with him.*

"Get off of me!" Gregory roared.

"Not until you hear me loud and clear Gregory. I'm not going anywhere until you stop acting like a lunatic. I don't want to be here either, but until I know that you are all right, I can't go. I love you that much to suffer through this little performance until you calm down." Phin stated.

"Love me? You don't even know me. When you walked through that door you thought Delia was Lily. You didn't even know or care for that matter, she was dead."

"I know my children like I know myself. I have grieved her loss same as you."

"Bullshit!"

"Bullshit, huh? Fine I'll prove it then." Phin bent his head closer to Gregory's ear despite his arm flailing almost hitting his face. "Your favorite book is Fahrenheit 451 and you read it every summer on the deck at sun down. You hate school but excel in your studies when forced. You like to run in the cold and try to do so every morning in the winter no matter what the weather. You are a Steelers fan and Lily rooted for the Browns. You two liked to fight often and left team memorabilia in each other's room or car until you shredded her signed vintage Bernie Kosar jersey and Nola put a stop to that. You two went skiing together every weekend when it snowed. I also know that she was pregnant when she died and a week later you lost your virginity. So as you can see, I know more about you than Nola."

"How can you possibly know all that stuff about us?" Gregory's body went limp with disbelief.

"I have the ability to decode a persons most recent

thoughts through their voice. All it takes is for someone to answer hello in a mobile message for me to gather information. I have kept not only an eye but an ear on you two from day one. Ask Nola. She would know when it was me and would purposely have one of you answer a device."

"All these years. Why didn't you say something?" Gregory panted. The weight of Phin pushing on him.

"Because, Gregory, before I left, your mother said not to come back until I could love you the way you deserve. I never thought I was capable."

"It's true Gregory. I saw it right before you tackled him." I looked at Phin and I added, "Can you please let him out of the headlock? I think he'll behave himself now."

Though I eyed, Gregory, still not totally sure. All the fighting was starting to wear on me and it wasn't even my family. My family barely existed anymore.

*Alone…Gregory I am so alone*, I thought. I could feel myself falling into a great sadness.

"Gregory can you take me home? I'm getting tired."

"Sure, sweets." He seemed to calm down though I knew the storm had not settled for those two though at least Phin cared more than he was letting on. The three of them would have to work it out amongst themselves. One thing I knew for sure, I couldn't release Phin in good conscience without Gregory getting the resolution he needed. As Phin had said, he would just have to suffer through it because he deserved every punch Gregory wanted to throw.

"No Greg, don't let her leave yet. She needs to meditate first."

"Excuse me." I glared at Phin unable to believe that man's nerve.

"She is very sad. She thinks she hasn't any family. She feels isolated from you right now. Not to mention my little act messed with her mind and for that, I do apologize Delia."

"Please Gregory, can we deal with this tomorrow?"

"Greg, she could hurt herself."

"Stop it! I've just had a really rough time lately."

"That is why you need us to look out for you." Gregory said in the no nonsense tone I hated.

"I am the leader and I want to go home." I stated giving direct eye contact to Phin.

"Well come on little leader. You can leave as soon as you get rid of all that negative energy you've just absorbed from us." Phin said as he bent down and picked me up while Gregory opened the sliding door.

Phin's presence was beginning to tick *me* off.

# CHAPTER 13

I'm not sure how long it took me to feel better, but I was interrupted by the sounds of Gregory's voice yelling, again. When I finally was at the top of the grand staircase, I expected to see Phin and Gregory going at it yet again. To my delight, I saw Luke bracing himself through the doorjamb as Gregory was attempting to throw him back outside.

"I just need to see her, man. I don't want to step on your toes trust me. She's a little young for my taste."

"Then why are you here, Silver Tongue?"

"My name is LUKE and I have to see Delia. Please let me in."

"Luke!" I said and Gregory released Luke when he saw my excitement.

"Delia, thank goodness!" He ran up the stairs and hugged me.

"How is Theresa?"

"She is perfect now thanks to you. All of her tests have come back completely clean. She is trying to convince my mom to let her go back to school."

Gregory yelled up to us with frustration thick enough to cut with a knife, "STOP TALKING IN SPANISH!".

"It's probably best if you let Gregory understand us. He has had a really bad day and I don't want him feeling alienated from our conversation anymore."

"What about the other one?"

"Oh you mean Phin? He's okay."

"I could do German next, get him really riled up."

"Hmm…tempting, but I think English will do. Can you speak any language?"

"Any spoken language."

"And you can make anyone you want understand you?"

"Groups if I wanted." Luke shrugged.

"I KNOW THAT'S GERMAN!" Gregory bellowed out through clenched teeth as he was turning purple.

"Please Luke, let Phin and Gregory in on what we're saying."

"Are you able to understand us now, kid?" Luke asked pointedly to Gregory.

"That's really nice to hear that about Theresa. How did you find me anyways?" I asked trying to get Luke's attention back by taking a hold of his sleeve and wiggling a little.

"I found your address in your chart. Your mom told me you were here so I walked."

"That's more than five miles - she couldn't give you a ride?"

"I like to walk."

"But I could have missed you. You could have been wandering around a strange city lost and I wouldn't have known."

"I had a good feeling that I'd find you." Luke smiled.

"How can you be so sure?"

"I don't know but it just felt right. The closer I got here, the less anxiety I was having."

"Have you had the chest pain then?" Phin inquired.

"Yeah how did you know? It's like a really a bad case of heart burn."

"AWW CRAP!" Gregory exclaimed with disgust.

"What is there some sort of airplane flu going around?" I wondered maybe Gregory's reaction was because he didn't want me to get sick.

"No Delia, he is one of us." Gregory looked pissed.

"This is insane!" I smiled then laughed.

"Come-On!" Gregory looked up as if praying. I looked down at him from the top of the steps realizing how handsome he was in his jealousy.

"You'll always be my guy." I looked directly into Gregory's eyes and he smiled a little sexy smile. Then the doorbell rang.

"Really? What is this, frickin' Grand Central Station?" Gregory grimaced as he answered the door and I laughed because he sounded like Nola. I really loved him, cranky and all.

Luke helped me down all fifteen steps of the grand staircase as Gregory opened the front door again to a short and stocky dark haired man.

"Can I help you?" Gregory growled slightly.

"Yes. May I speak to Delia?" He asked in a tone like he and I had an appointment. It was his assertiveness that made me walk closer with interest.

"I'm Delia." I stated before Gregory could turn him away.

"Ah, so the Delia Distraction has a face with the phenomena." He added.

"I'm sorry?"

"That's what the headlines are saying in the Carolinas. Your performance, and to be specific your disappearance, has caused quite a rumble."

"How am I considered a distraction?" I asked in genuine curiosity. "You have created an obsession among our viewers. They are demanding more about you. You have become their beacon of hope."

"I'm sorry Mr.?" Gregory interjected.

"Spada, Manny Spada."

"Well Mr. Spada, I'm sorry but we can't help you. You have the wrong person. Delia is a very common name." Gregory began to close the door when the little man shoved himself back through.

"No I don't think I do. You see I do my homework and there was only one Delia in St. Demetrius's Hospital database. Although I couldn't get a last name because of privacy regulations. I was able to get the nurse's name that had her as his charge, a Luke Cantalano." This was too much for Gregory he picked up the little man by the front of his shirt and was now in his face.

"Now listen here, you little worm. You have made a mistake. You will go home now and find some other story to report on."

I could see Gregory concentrating, trying to sway the man's thoughts, but I knew Manny Spada was thinking clearly. He wasn't even slightly afraid. Gregory's power couldn't cloud his mind enough for Manny Spada to go home.

"You think I'm afraid of you, Sasquatch? I have been doing this job before you were a tadpole." With that he kicked Gregory between the legs and twisted his body from Gregory's grip.

"Now that was uncalled for, don't you think?" Phin stood next to Gregory helping him up.

"And who are you?" Manny looked like he was readying another kick.

"The tadpole's father and friend to Delia. I haven't known her very long, but she might not want to talk to you if you beat up her friends."

"Please, honey," Manny was trying to peer around my protectors. "If you would only give me a few minutes. I have traveled all day long following the nurse around. I only want to ease the viewers' curiosity."

"Let's go sit in the library. I will consider answering your questions one by one as you ask them. Understood?" I was proud of how confident I was being.

"Of course." Manny smiled.

As we sat he talked to someone on his mobile. Miranda

showed up with a brush and raked it through my frizzy hair.

"How do I look?" I asked Gregory while looking up at him as he stood behind me.

"Gorgeous as always." He said out loud and then whispered in my ear. "Are you sure you want to do this?"

"Yeah, I really don't think you should." Luke spoke and I looked up at both of them.

"I agree with Silver Tongue. Even though he is the one who led him here."

And then Phin walked over putting a hand on his son's shoulder and added, "We could just kick the spunky little guy out and close the door. If that's what you want Delia? We could just get rid of him." Phin shrugged.

"Listen you three, do you think pissing this guy off isn't going to stop him from coming with others next time? Maybe if I give him the interview, this will become yesterdays news if the mystery is gone."

"I hope you are right." Gregory whispered as he kissed my ear and they sat in front of Manny.

I really didn't know if I was making the right decision. I felt like doing nothing was just going to exacerbate the situation.

"Are you ready?" Manny asked not hearing our conversation.

"Yes," I said.

"I'm sorry? I didn't get that. Was that a yes?"

"I am ready when you are."

"Can you speak English please? I'm bilingual, but I don't know anything other that Spanish and English." Manny was getting frustrated.

I looked to Luke and he shrugged. "Are you sure about this?" His said from across the room. "I feel responsible for this whole situation."

"Why don't we start with that language you're speaking? What is it?" Manny glared at Luke.

"Mandarin," Luke said to Manny and then addressed me. "Delia?"

"I know everything is as it should be," I said to Luke and he nodded.

"Ok Mr. Spada, shall we begin?" I asked.

"Manny, call me Manny."

"Hit me with your best shot Manny."

"Did you heal Theresa Hernandez and how?"

"Wow, you don't beat around the bush do you?"

"Well I'm really not sure how long I have before your wolf pack decides to either throw me out or eat me alive?" Then I felt his fear and I immediately grabbed his hand.

"You have my word that you can ask as many questions as you like and I will answer them honestly. If for some reason I don't like your question, I'll just ask you to rephrase it." I let his fear flood into me hoping to ease his nerves. "So to answer your first question: Yes I believe I did and I really don't know how. I guess with a gift from the universe or maker. Whatever works best for you."

"Are you in some sort of organized religion?" Which made me smile because I knew what he was getting at.

"I do not belong to any religion or cult."

"God's prophets often are peddling a bible of some sort? Can I buy a copy? Or is it free as long I agree to work in your commune?" Manny smirked.

"Commune?"

"Your wolf pack?"

He pointed to the guys and I couldn't help but laugh. The Cross House a commune? Though the more I thought about it I guess it did look like the guys and Miranda were my followers. I was glad Nola was napping so she couldn't be drawn into this craziness. What he must of thought when Miranda brushed my hair. Yikes! I was going to have to stay calm and turn this conversation around.

"So you don't think that I healed Luke's sister?"

"No. I think that you influenced both Theresa and Zoey into believing you are some sort of healer when you're just a very good actress. Or maybe you are a hypnotist? The chemotherapy must have been working and you just happen to come along with your little performance. What I don't understand is why you ran away?"

"I was discharged."

"You didn't want to reap the reward?"

"What reward is that?" I asked.

"The glory of convincing those what you can do so you can get your fifteen minutes of fame. Maybe even be able to pick up a few more followers." I was still holding his hand not letting him pull away. I started to mentally finger through his past as if paging through an old book, looking for just the right vision.

"Hmm…your mother is very upset with you. She has never liked that you became a reporter. You wouldn't let them activate an ear clip. Why?"

"Oh you're a psychic too what a surprise!" Manny said sarcastically, "I know what a cold read is, when I see one."

"You have a hobby…a secret hobby you are embarrassed about. You like to dress up for Star Trek conventions using the name Plaque."

"The new shows are super popular now. I did a piece on it a while back. Also, it's easy to see because I'm short, I would make an excellent Ferengi."

"Nothing I say will convince you?"

"Probably not." Manny said and Luke jumped up.

"Excuse me sir. Do you have a pocket knife in your little belt of tools?" Luke asked. Manny started to rummage through his bag until he found a red Swiss army knife. I suddenly knew what Luke was up to. I simultaneously dropped Manny's hand and grabbed Luke's.

"Please don't do this?" I begged.

"I have to Dee, he is making fun of my most favorite person."

"But I don't know if I can make it work all the time."

"I know everything is as it should be." He parroted back to me letting me know that he had faith greater than my own.

"Oh good more drama." Manny put his arms up waving his hands with the open knife in it. "What is it we are going to do with the knife? Put Delia on a wheel, spin her around and throw it at her. That would make this the circus and I haven't been to one in such a long time."

"Would You Shut-Up!" Luke yelled as he grabbed Manny's hand with the opened knife and shoved it into his side. Manny froze as Luke's blood gushed on to his hand and the floor. I knew that the warmth was undeniable, Manny had to know that Luke was actually hurt. Then there was a smell of raw sewage.

"Why did you do that?" Manny cried his face stricken in horror, "You punctured your large intestine. If we don't get you to a hospital fast you'll die from sepsis. Is she really worth risking death?"

Luke looked right into my eyes. "Yes, she is."

Gregory helped me kneel down next to him. I couldn't feel my legs because of the fear pulsing through my body. Please work, I prayed.

"You could have just sliced your hand you know." I mumbled to Luke.

"It wouldn't have been enough. We had to make sure that Manny knows you're the real thing. It was his knife and his own hand that stabbed me. Manny was in the Dome Wars and knows how fatal this kind of wound is. I saw a report he did once about it."

I placed my hands on his abdomen and immediately felt the warm in them without even trying and I knew that a seizure would soon follow.

And that was the day I came out to the world with my gift. Not with words, but a circus performance that Manny had never before seen.

*I hope he got his money's worth*, I thought.

"Ask Phin about the five golden rings. He gave one to my mom." I heard Lily say as the blackness took over.

"Delia Stanton wake up." A sing-songy little girls voice surrounded me. "If you don't wake up, how are you going to put that man in his place."

"Oh shut-up! I'm tired." I growled.

"Then sleep my beautiful girl. We'll work it out with your mom." It was Nola's voice now and not the same little girl voice I heard at first.

"I'm sorry Nola. I was dreaming. Where is Manny?"

"Downstairs still but you don't have to resume that silly interview."

"I think I'm supposed to. I'm actually thinking that he was sent here for a reason."

"Okay, honey, calm down. I'll bring him up to you."

When he arrived at the door, he seemed unsure with his camera in hand. He wanted his story but he also was scared out of his wits. His feelings pumped through me as I reach out willingly for a connection with Manny Spada. He sat uneasily in the chair near the bed.

"So your skepticism has turned into a big ball of fear. I won't hurt you Manny. Why are you really here? Is it really to prove that the hope others are experiencing is just bunk?" I smiled as Nola's vocabulary came out of my mouth.

"I would call it delusional thinking which in my experienced is never a good thing."

"So now you have fallen into the delusion. What is it now? Am I a hypnotist?"

"I can't be hypnotized Delia. I am not the right mark and if you were a fake you would know that already."

"So where do we go from here?"

"I don't know. I think I'll just set up the camera and let you talk this time because without an angle to work from, I am lost."

"Well then I guess we should get started, if you want

this for the morning segment." I looked directly into the camera then back at Manny again. Now I was scared. The words I was about to say I knew were important. They had nothing really to do with me but those who were observing. It was their hopes and dreams that were at stake. I needed to make my first dent and I didn't know how.

"What is your full name and where are you from?"

"Delia Hazel Stanton. I am a homegrown Clevelander."

"Why did you go to the Coastal District and how did you get to be in the hospital?"

"I was there to visit friends and I suffered from an illness that caused me to run high fevers and have seizures."

"How were you able to heal Theresa Hernandez?"

"I think it's a gift to help us. I don't know how it works. When I touched her, my hands got really hot. Then I noticed that her bruises from her leukemia were gone. It was the first time that I was aware of what was happening and I'm not sure how much control I have over this gift."

"Why aren't you shocked by this gift's onset?"

"It is not my first. I have two others. I am also an empath and a psychic."

"Why were you chosen to have these gifts?"

"We all have these gifts, I think, to help us find our callings. If we are quiet enough and follow the path that is presented, you can find happiness here."

"When you say we, are you suggesting that everyone has gifts inside them, even me?"

"Yes, your gift is truth. Some search and can never find it. You, however have the ability to see the truth in a situation even if you don't like it. You still will always know what is right and what is wrong."

"I'm sorry?"

"You kept pushing downstairs until you got the truth. As long as you keep digging, the truth will always find you."

"Why did you leave like you did?"

"I just wanted to avoid this situation."

"So you don't want to be involved with the media?"

"I don't think there is a choice with savvy reporters out there like you."

"Well I'm sure I'm just the beginning and I hope you'll keep us informed at First News Coastal about all your current endeavors."

"I don't think I will officially talk to anyone else, but thank you, Manny."

"Well thank you, for this."

"You're very welcome." I said, as he then turned off his device and began to gather himself for departure.

# CHAPTER 14

As I progressed in my recovery, I waited for more reporters. One week went by then the next and I was walking well enough to return to school. Normally after missing a month I would have been behind, but with the help of Gregory's tutor, Perry, I was completely caught up and prepared to take finals in June. I was studying for a Chemistry test when my mom called me to the family room.

"Do you have something to tell me?" She frowned.

"Huh?" Then I saw my face on the screen and I knew this was going to be interesting. My little segment had trickled on up to our local stations.

"When did you do this and what are you talking about having gifts and such? This is unacceptable, Delia. Going behind my back without even telling me. Talking fairytales to reporters. I have a job you know. What should I tell my boss? My daughter has the imagination of a five year old and she is just out of her mind!" She ranted.

I knew this would happen and I was prepared for it. I let her finish. I also intended to have my say.

"You have always known that there was something different about me, Mom. Dad embraced it while you felt the need to hide it. I can't help what's happening and I will do my best to keep you out of it but this is who I am. Gregory has shown me the importance of using what you have been given otherwise you deserve the misery you wallow in."

"I'm not miserable."

"I know, but I was, because you couldn't support what I was becoming."

"I think you should see someone, Delia. I may have failed you in the past, but I can help you now."

"I don't need to be helped! I need you to accept things the way they are. You let me know if I should pack my bags or not."

With that I left the room. My throat was closing from held back tears and I didn't want to show any weakness. I needed her to know I was confident and not some irrational teen.

I left a very tart note to avoid another confrontation and took my bike to school early. The cool spring air was thin and it was easy to maneuver, even though I was a little unsteady for my first ride since the trip.

I went to my empty locker and unloaded the contents of my bag. I had an hour till the bell rang. I went to find a quiet place to study. I heard some seniors talking ahead and it didn't even occur to me to avoid them. I walked past them like I always did with the knowledge I was a ghost in their little world. It didn't bother me. I preferred it.

*Why was Winter and her bright blond head, walking in my path?* I wondered. *Whatever.*

I walked on the opposite side and as she passed with the three others, she grabbed the back of my ponytail propelling me into the girls bathroom door. The three others shoved me through so hard that my body landed on its side upon the cold hard floor. I lay there unsure what was happening.

"Get up!" Winter commanded and I did what I was told, too stunned to say anything. "Do you have any idea how much you've embarrassed us?" She continued.

"Excuse me? I forgot your name." I said sarcastically.

"I wish I didn't know yours." Winter scowled.

"Good. Pretend you don't, so I can leave."

I went to leave and Winter shoved me down again.

"You're not getting off that easily! You have no idea what I have lost! I had an Academy boy in my sights and his father KNOWS people. One party and I could have been in. Now he texts me that he can't be seen going out with someone from the freak school."

"Too bad, it sounds like you two we're perfect for each other." I said as I rolled my eyes.

"Well since you have made me into a freak now, I must make you look like one officially. Sweet Tea, give me something that can cut!" Her lackey pulled out a plastic knife from the cafeteria.

"This is all I have." Sweat Tea offered.

"What can I do with that exactly?"

"Maybe if you spread butter on your inner thighs, that Academy guy will give you the time again." I regretted that as soon as I said it. My anger toward my mother was coming out. I was kicking a snapping puppy.

"GO FIND ME SOMETHING ELSE!" Winter screamed. Sweet Tea ran out and came back to my regret with a pair of humungous fabric scissors.

*Why did the Home EC room have to be right next door?* I whined to myself in my head.

Sweet Tea grabbed a chair from the hall and Blondie and no name sat me down in it. I did try to struggle, but I still had some muscle weakness and gave up quickly.

Winter grabbed my hair, yanking until I yelped. She laughed and then said, "I haven't even begun."

Now I was afraid, not because she was going to cut my hair. I just had a vision of all three of them lying dead on the floor and me on my knees crying. Winter started cutting. Grabbing yanking cutting, grabbing yanking cutting.

*Why would I kill them? It was only hair?* I thought.

I looked at my stands of reddish-brown falling into my lap. I suddenly surged forward from the intense pain as the scissors sliced into my right ear lobe causing the blood to drip onto my shirt in a little steam.

"Wow these things cut skin pretty good." Winter cackled.

"Please stop. You don't know what you're doing." I pleaded.

"Oh on the contrary, I think I'm doing a super job."

The fear was taking over and I was losing control. There was something growing inside me. This is the flip side, the opposite of healing. It was breaking. Like breaking every bone in their bodies including their skulls. There was a part of me that wanted to kill them. Gregory said I would learn to control my ability. I wasn't twenty yet. Self-preservation was kicking in and I didn't know if I could stop it.

"I think we should even out those lobes." Winter whispered in my still perfect ear.

My brain was targeting them like a video game Gregory always played. Placing a point on top of each head and then linking up the points. If she cut me again, I wouldn't be able to stop it.

*Focus, must focus on something else.*

"Gregory, please help!" I cried in my thoughts knowing I was lost. Suddenly, I was at Nola's kitchen table watching Gregory work with Perry his tutor.

"Delia? Why are you here. You're supposed to be at school?"

"Greg man, who are you talking to? She's not here."

"Help Gregory I need you. I might kill them." I yelled.

Then I was back with the girls. This time, instead of it being an accident she was deliberately putting the teeth of the scissors up high so that she could get a bigger chunk this time.

*What can I do to prevent this? There must be something I can do to stop me from killing them.*

I have two other powers maybe they had flip sides that weren't so lethal. Psychic visions could help me. Yes maybe

I could use the projection of the healing/breaking and empath ability to project to push my emotional and physical pain at them. I had to do it quickly. Winter was getting her nerve back. I knew she wasn't going to back down with her lackeys there. First, she had to get up her nerve because cutting someone on accident is a lot different than on purpose. It takes a choice to hurt someone intentionally and this was her first time. Well, physically, at least enough to draw blood. Nola told me once that intentionally hurting someone changes the soul and can shift your path.

I kept seeing me watching as their skulls were being crushed. Pain, I had to focus on just the empath ability of feeling pain. Just pain. I needed to flip it not to me, just them. Not me just them. I targeted then fired.

At first it was a subtle buzzing nothing to even rub away. Then I saw an imaginary dial in my mind. I walked over and turned it up. I heard three bodies hit the floor behind me.

"No," I cried and jumped up, no longer being held down by Winter's accomplices.

Though this time was different than the vision. This time they were breathing and their bodies didn't looked like they had been run over by a semi truck. Relief past over me till I realized I had only one option now, RUN. I turned to get out the door when a female janitor came through the door foiling my last option.

Sitting in the principal's office as Gregory showed up first and then my mother, I was many things: embarrassed, wordless, scared and the list could go on. When my mother entered the room, anger filled me making me one messed up little empath.

"Why is my daughter here when clearly, whatever happened, she was defending herself? She is bleeding for goodness sakes!"

"Mrs. Stanton I have been made aware of the situation. The other girls and their parents have agreed not to get the police involved if you don't."

"Police really? I will show you police! If I hear one inkling about police I will have my lawyer suing the pants off of all of you. And if this happens again I will sue for sure!"

"It is my recommendation that Delia not come back to classes here at this time."

"You're expelling her!" My mother seethed.
"No, of course not, but it would appear that Delia is not capable of attending without some sort of jealousy from the others since she has become…um…famous. It would be best for her protection as well as the others. Also that was another condition the girls' parents presented to me."

"What, do they give money to the football team?" Mom said. Normally I would say mom was being irrational. By the look on the principal's face, not to mention the guilty feelings that I could practically smell, she was spot on.

"I really think that we should stick to the point." He cleared his throat. "Delia should find a tutor for the end of the school year at the very least until her little problem is resolved."

"She can study with me. Perry is first rate." Gregory interjected from the door his voice commanding his wishes to all of us.

"Yes. Maybe that would be for the best." My mom said first completely taken in.

"Definitely!" Principle Foster agreed of course unnecessarily.

"For sure!" I said before shaking off the haze enough to turn and glare at Gregory.

The three of them followed me as I cleaned out my locker again. This time I took all my personal items, well basically just one item; a small poster of Tag That Kid in concert at Madison Square Garden. I was allowed to take my books for now until after finals. On the way to the car, I stopped my mom, who was on her way back to work.

While I was supposed to resume back with Perry that very afternoon, sore ear and all.

"Thanks, mom, for sticking up for me back there." I called after her and she turned sharply.

"You listen here. I defended you only because I was trying to piece back somewhat of a normal life for you. I guess that is not going to happen is it Delia?"

"No mom it won't." I sighed.

"I'm sorry, I can't do this. I just don't understand you. I was given an opportunity recently and after this incident today, I've decided to take it. My boss wants me in Portland for the next few months, and I leave tomorrow. Normally I would have you stay with family, but to tell you the truth, I don't think THEY would even take you right now. Since you are going to be getting your studies at Nola's, I'm going to ask her if she will take you on."

"Ok, momma," A lone tear trickled down my cheek and the pain grew in my throat.

If I could measure on a scale of emotional pain I have felt in my life, I would say this matched up to losing my Dad pretty damn close.

# CHAPTER 15

Abandonment didn't suit me. I was an orphan, and that was all that I could think over and over again. I thought about following my mom to Portland, telling her that I loved her and would do anything to make this right again. When I got there I knew I wouldn't be convincing because it wasn't true. I knew I was supposed to remain here in Cleveland and here I would stay. Although, it didn't stop me from hating myself for not measuring up to what she needed me to be. I was falling into a great depression and unable to let go of the perfect image she wanted. I found myself detaching into numbness.

So I ignored the other side of me, the side that wanted me to change. I didn't want to feel everybody's pain anymore. I couldn't even deal with my own pain. I was afraid of what's unnatural.

*I am a danger to the people I love*, I thought to myself. And that's when I descended into the numbness, hiding away from even Gregory.

"Get up, Delia!" Gregory said.

I had been staying at Gregory's for three days. I wouldn't let anyone comfort me. I wouldn't even let Miranda fix my hair. The zigzags from the fabric scissors were my punishment. I deserved them in my opinion.

"Go away!" I yelled at him.

"Come on, you have to at least eat."

"Can't I just sleep? Isn't that what a guest is supposed

to do. You know, relax."

"You haven't ever been a guest here. Now come on. Nola made you pancakes. You'll hurt her feelings if you don't come downstairs."

I sat there with all of them staring at me. Luke looked especially worried, but I wasn't sure because I was happily numb. He had gotten a job pretty quickly at the Cleveland Clinic as a PRN. They called and ask him if he could work when they had a call off. He had the need to stay with me the same as Phin. I'm guessing Nola, Gregory and Miranda would have it too if they left the city. I needed to find out how to release them because I wasn't worth it. I hadn't figured out what needed to be done on July seventh or what five golden rings meant. And I wasn't in the mood to ask Phin about anything. I knew that would open another can of worms. Although I'd have to get off my ass and do something. I was running out of time.

"Do you want another, hon?" Nola asked but I was distracted by the radio's irritating song.

When you're smiling

When you're smiling

The whole world smiles with you

"Huh?" I finally responded.

"Would you like another pancake?" Nola asked with the pan in her hand.

"Uh…no." I responded and Phin shot a look at me.

When you're laughing

When you're laughing

The sun comes shining through

"Could someone please turn off that stupid song?"

"Song?" Nola asked.

"Yeah. The radio, can you change the channel?"

But when you're crying

You bring on the rain

So quit you're sighing and be happy again.

"AAH…never mind I'll do it myself." I said with hostility.

"What are you talking about?" Gregory said with his eyebrows bunched together.

I stomped over the radio and went to push the off button. Then I realized it wasn't on. The song continued about wanting me to be happy.

"Shut up, shut up, shut up." I yelled into the air.

"Delia, what is going on?" Gregory asked as every one of them gave me a concerned face and then rose from their seats.

"We don't hear anything." Miranda stepped forward.

"Well, I'm not crazy, it's coming from somewhere. Phin tell them you hear that."

"All I hear is that you're irritated by something. That and you want to find a way to release us, because you don't know what we're supposed to do on July seventh so you're giving up." Then Phin turned to Gregory.

*He didn't mention the five golden rings?*

"She's losing it. We need to get her help quickly."

"I'm not losing anything." Gosh, Melanie wasn't this annoying and she could actually read thoughts. Unlike 'Mr. I'm the Man,' Phin, decoding half the stuff I'm thinking and then filling in the other unsaid side as he goes.

*Yeah Melanie…*

"Where are you going?" Phin demanded.

"Don't mind me. I'm nuts, remember?"

I went to text Melanie asking her what was up and if she could come over. She said sure, I think because she was a little curious about me. I had been keeping in touch with her the whole time since I left, telling her that I was all right but wouldn't be back to work because of an accident. She, of course had tons of questions, which I avoided. She was there within twenty minutes, which was not soon enough for me. My guardians had a sharp eye making sure I didn't run down the street stark naked singing some crazy song that only came from inside my head.

The song continued to play over and over in a loop as if waiting for me to act on whatever I was supposed to do. When I went to answer the door, I realized I couldn't hear it anymore.

"You've got to be kidding me." I yelled psychotically again.

"What's wrong and what the hell happened to your hair?" I explained to her the song that I heard in the kitchen that no one else could. I completely avoided talking about my hair.

"They think I'm nuts and now I can't hear it anymore. You must think I'm crazy too."

"Where did you hear it last?" I walked towards the kitchen with the whole group following. And I heard it again. Melanie closed her eyes and started singing the tune.

"I love that song. My nana used to sing it to cheer me up. Though I like Frank Sinatra's version that's Louie Armstrong."

"HA! YOU DO HEAR IT!" I danced, immaturely pointing Phin. When I was done, I sobered with, "Well I need to turn it off otherwise I will go nuts."

She walked around listening to my vision. She put her ear to the wall. "It's coming from this wall."

"What's above?" I demanded from Nola.

"I don't know - the hallway?" She shrugged. I ran upstairs with everyone following. The sound was still in the wall but this time it was louder. I immediately ran down the long hall past Lily's room to the stairwell then to the meditation room. Stopping at the top, I had a hard time catching my breath at what I saw. The whole room was filled with people dancing and enjoying themselves.

"Wow," Melanie said, marveling at what she saw. Then I saw it, something that wasn't there in my time, a second elevator. The music must have been resonating down the shaft all the way through the kitchen wall. I tried to enter it by pulling open the door, but it was no use. It didn't exist where I was so I couldn't manipulate it. Then it moved going down where I couldn't go. Angrily I hit it with my fist only to feel wall, not metal. After a few minutes, it came up with two men holding wooden crates filled with glass bottles. They walked over to the bar going behind it, restocking for their thirsty guests.

"I was getting worried!" said the man at the bar very loudly. "I was thinking I'd have to go home sober." Everyone around him laughed merrily.

Then the song ended and everything restarted again. I was supposed to see something else but what? I scanned the room looking for something else then I saw them; Aunt Helen and Juniper holding hands walking to the elevator.

"I put them all down here, Helen." She and Helen walked into the elevator and the vision ended.

"Wow you HAVE to call me every time that happens. That was awesome," Melanie exclaimed.

"I have to get through this wall. There was an elevator here once. Nola, I need a sledgehammer."

"Yeah, let's give her a sledgehammer. Who thinks that's a good idea?" Phin laughed.

I looked at them and they all still had unsure looks on their faces. What the hell? I had a couple bad days and now I lost all credibility. Phin was not helping.

"Come on, guys! I called Melanie here to convince you. She believes me and she doesn't know the whole story yet."

"You have been a zombie for almost a week. I hear from your own thoughts that you are basically abandoning us, including my son. Then a second later, you are calling someone I never met and following hallucinations around the house. Now you want a sledgehammer. Are you going do us in or what Delia?"

"Gregory, please, this is right I know it." I begged.

"Have faith in me. I'm sorry for turning my back on you."
I turned to him then back to all of them. "In fact, I apologize
to all of you. My own mother didn't believe in me, so I was
thinking why should I. But this is right, trust me, Nola. Let me
break through this wall and if there is nothing there. I'll check
myself into a clinic."

"Gregory, go to the workbench in the cellar and see
what you can find."

He was back quickly with two ball pine hammers and
a crowbar and went right for the wall. Luke joined in helping
without question. They broke through about the size of a beach
ball revealing a brick wall.

"No it can't be. It is here. You saw it too.
Didn't you, Mel?"

"Yes, Delia I did. I saw what was happening
in your mind."

"You too now! It has to be here."

"She's cracking under pressure. Time to put her in the
shop, Greg." Phin started laughing again. Gregory rushed him
pushing him to the ground.

"If Delia says there was an elevator, then there was.
It's okay, Delia, we'll figure it out." He took me by the shoulders
and led me away from the wall, but I ran towards it touching
the brick and I saw her. It was Juniper crying sitting on the
ground putting the bricks in place. She was saying goodbye
to her best friend and her dream of changing the world
for the better.

"What if your best friend left you and you were
suffering from postpartum depression? Without Helen, Juniper
felt like a fraud and sealed all her dreams up, and at the same
time burying her pain. Nola how did you find out about
the Alignment?"

"From a journal my mother left me. She saw I would be
married soon. I met your grandfather very soon after and we
were married. You see she never talked about the Alignment of

Kairos when she was alive. Sure, she would do the occasional palm reading, but never acted serious about her gift. I was twenty and it was a week after she died from cancer when I found the journal."

"It is here." I touched the wall with both hands focusing. I needed to break through. No, I wanted to pulverize the brick. I closed my eyes and thought of a cut out doorway, creating boundary lines because I didn't want to accidentally bring the whole house down. Before I knew it, bricks were crumbling along with the rest of the drywall. I put my hand though a hole trying to feel for something and I grasped a metal gate. I shook it hard. "You see, it's there!"

It took me about an hour to remove all the brick until I stepped back and marveled at it. It existed! I couldn't believe it myself. There it was uncovered after being entombed for more than seventy years. I went to open the gate and Gregory stopped me.

"What are you doing?"

"I need to go down there."

"Sorry Sweets, you're going to have to wait. You can't just get on an old elevator without having it checked out."

"AH! What the hell?" I couldn't control my frustration.

"Relax. I know you're feeling the pull and I know it's undeniable. It's how I found you the first day, but you have to realize these old cables could snap. There probably isn't any electricity connected to it, anyway."

"Call someone now and get it working." Gregory touched his ear clip and found the mobile code. It was whoever took care of the other elevator's maintenance.

Melanie walked with me to my room as we waited for the elevator repair guy to come. We talked about all the questions she had that I was avoiding, even my hair.

"You have to get that fixed." Mel said.

"Yeah, I guess I should." I sighed. "Miranda wanted to. I was thinking I was a freak, so I deserved to look like one."

"That's just crazy. Just because someone imposes their point of view on you doesn't mean it's true, you know."

"Yeah, I guess so."

"You have this big purpose you have to fulfill. That can be pretty scary for someone so young. Give yourself a break."
I didn't know what to say after a long pause she continued with, "Gregory seems pretty awesome. I met a guy."

"What's he like?" I smiled.

"You'll meet him when you come back to work."

"Really. You still want me?"

"Sure," Mel laughed. "It's not like you ditched work on purpose. You were sick."

Again another long pause. It was like I was so soul sick. I couldn't keep the conversation going.

She finally said, "I'm going to go get Miranda and we'll fix that hair."

Melanie could make herself at home anywhere and you always wanted to welcome her with open arms. She was the kind of person you didn't have to entertain. She could pull her own rabbit from her own hat and she always did.

They made a fuss over me by painting my nails and cutting my hair and did my face with a little makeup. Miranda was especially careful around my ears knowing that I needed a little handholding. She must have been able to feel my fear with her empath ability. She whispered what she was doing with every step. Melanie was in charge of my nails and makeup, which I never really cared about.

When they were done I scrutinized my new look in the full-length mirror. I had never had my hair so short. The way it laid around my ears with my long nose and high cheekbones gave me kind an elfish look. I never saw myself as breakable, but that is how I looked, delicate. I ran to the bathroom and got on the scale. It was my weight. I had lost twenty pounds the past year and didn't even realize it.

Sure my size had changed, but different clothing

stores have different sizes and I just thought when I worked at Fabulous Fashions that their clothes ran bigger. That wasn't the case. Looking at myself in the mirror, I was completely enthralled. By changing the inside, I had gradually changed the outside, too. I was a brand new person. I wasn't a freak at all. I wouldn't change a thing. I liked me.

# CHAPTER 16

"Where is he, Gregory?" I whined.

"He'll be here this afternoon."

"I'm sorry. I don't get why he would say he is coming one day and then calls to say he can't make it until the next."

"Relax. When you come home from work, it will be fixed."

"No one goes down there until I get home. Got it?"

"You know the guy that fixes it has to ride the lift?"

"Whatever, only him then. How much do you trust this guy?"

"He has been fixing our other one for a while. I don't know. Do you want me to frisk him before he goes?"

"No, Smartass, but I think you should keep an eye on him. Make sure he doesn't take anything no matter how minuscule."

"Not even a flea shall be taken, My Lady."

"You are a complete weirdo."

"Yes, but I'm your complete weirdo and never forget it."

"I have to go. That's Mel. I'll be back at four," I said after hearing her horn honk in the drive.

"I won't move from this very spot until you return, My Lady. You are the sunlight in the sky; the raindrop in-"

I closed the door on Sir Smarty Pants before I threw something at him. Why do guys expect your full attention when they're serious but when you are focused on something, then they're all jokes. I had the feeling I'd one day figure out the mysteries of the universe and still be unable understand their stupid secret society of testosterone.

"You're preaching to the choir, sister," Melanie said, as I got into the car without even saying a word to her. "Did your elevator man come?"

"I can't even go there right now."

"I hope it's like a treasure trove of a 1920s wardrobe. Did I ever tell you I want to open a vintage clothing store one day?" I let her ramble on about how clothes totally lost their originality once they weren't sewn by hand. When we got to the store, the day wouldn't go quick enough, no matter how much I tried to keep busy. I kept looking at the time on my ear clip.

"So tell me about your guy, Mel," I asked, desperate for a distraction. "How can you date knowing everything he's thinking? You must go insane over the crap that's in the male mind." I was still a little annoyed with Gregory.

"Didn't I tell you? I can't hear Henry's thoughts for some reason."

My stomach twisted.

"Whoa, has that ever happened before?"

"No and I totally love it. I have never been more at peace in his arms without all the background noise. It's great, like he was born just to suit me."

*Or he was never born at all*, I thought.

"What's that supposed to mean?" Melanie frowned.

"I'm not sure. I'm sorry. I think I'm really tired."

*Why couldn't she hear him? There was something off. She was able to hear me and I had more abilities than most. Who the hell was he? Or what?*

"DELIA, what is your problem today?" She glared.

"I can't help it, Mel. Did you ever tell him you are a telepath?"

"What does that have to do with anything?"

"You told me right away the very second we met. If you haven't told him, then you probably don't trust him."

"You know, if you are going to be in this bad mood all day, you can leave early."

"I can't, you drove me." I really hated making her feel this way. She obviously really liked him but ignoring her own intuition was blinding her. I wished I could have just investigated him on my own without upsetting her like this.

"I am not upset. I have to go in the back to get, to get-" But I interpreted her with my thoughts:

*-to get yourself together. You know I'm right.*

She stormed off. I really cared for Melanie and if she deserved anything it was the truth. Especially, if she wasn't going to listen to her own inner voice screaming that there was anger. I didn't need a vision to tell me that.

We arrived back at the house and Melanie's disposition had not improved. We had to wait to pull into the drive because the elevator repair guy was leaving. Melanie and I looked at each other and then rushed from the old Vapor to get inside.

"Oh, so you're staying now are you?" I said as I smack her hand from the front doors old brass handle.

"I need to ask Miranda about a new hairstyle I'm thinking of getting."

*Yeah, right, she is just nosey as all hell.*

"Whatever, busybody." She didn't respond because she wanted to come in and if that meant taking a few jabs, so be it.

"Gregory? Nola? I'm home..." I yelled. Not one person came and Nola always greeted me.

I rushed up the stairs down the long hall and then ran up the back staircase with Melanie on my heels the whole way. Clearing through the door they all encircled the old elevator staring at it in wonder.

"I'm sure not going down there. Maintenance guy or not!" I heard Phin say.

"That's fine because I promised Delia we'd-"
He stopped as he saw me approaching.

"I'm ready. Let's go." I smiled.

"No, Delia. I think I should go first on my own."
Gregory frowned.

"Oh, no, we are all going, including Phin. This little
adventure is for all of us to share. If you are going to stay
Phin, then participate, otherwise I'll find a way to release you
because I'm getting tired of your demanding attitude."

I was yelling the same intentions in my head so he got it
from both ends my mind and my mouth. Phin and Mel both
glared at me and rubbed their foreheads.

"I'll go first by myself then you can go each three at a
time." Gregory looked as if he was about to argue but the
thought better of it. "Here?" He tossed me a flashlight before
I could close the gate. "The guy said it was pretty dark
down there."

He kept eye contact the whole time as I was submerged
into darkness. I didn't turn it on until I hit the bottom. I reveled
in the anticipation and fear. Then I sent it back up and turned to
face the darkness of a narrow cave.

"Holy crap," came from my mouth involuntary and
echoed the chamber.

Even though Gregory would want me to wait, I couldn't.
I was being pulled by that unknown force to complete this part
of the mission. I heard the rush of water above me, but
I couldn't see the source of only drips and drops here and there.

Helen appeared in her usual way, being dragged by Juniper.

"Here it is, Helen dear. It's for our children and our
children's children, their legacy. Behind this very door not even
James knows the combination. I was able to set it myself.
It took me a little a research on vault doors, I'll tell you.
It's worth it for security purposes. You and I are the only ones
in the whole world who can open it."

"Why would I know the combination already?"

"You remember the song we made up. The one we used to sing with the numbers in it."

And the vision ended.

"No!" I yelled ignoring the echo. "Comeback! I don't know the song." I pounded on the door wishing I had a crow bar. I tried to pulverize it. There wasn't any effect on solid steel.

"What is it, Delia?" Gregory bounded toward me the others in tow. "Are you hurt?"

"Besides the fact I could go insane trying to finish this one quest. How am I going to change the world when I can't even get through a man-made vaulted door?"

"We'll find a way. Maybe if we continue on down the corridor, we'll find a clue." Gregory said.

"Juniper and Helen only knew it. It was some song they made up with numbers in it. Nola did your mother ever sing you songs? Anything maybe your friends didn't recognize?"

"No just the usual nursery rhymes."

"I need three numbers from 1-99."

"Can we get out of here?" Phin peered around Nola.

"It's not his fault. He's claustrophobic." Miranda whispered into my ear.

We followed the path to the end where the sound of rushing water grew louder. In front of us stood a large steel door with a latch. Phin, Luke and Gregory pulled on it, jostling it loose until it would turn and open. We found ourselves behind the waterfall.

"It's the falls from the stream on the beach," Nola said.

After we were all through, I let the heavy door slam to reveal the back of it was rock that was stuccoed to the other side. When closed, there wasn't a visible seam and the door locked automatically.

"You wouldn't even know it was there," Luke said.

"I think that was the idea," Gregory replied, rolling his eyes.

"I don't think I'm in the mood for you two and your bickering today." I said, walking through the side of the falls trying not to slip. Nola was better at it then I was. I made a mental note to practice Tai Chi with her more often.

Everyone sat at the dining room table quietly waiting for my next move. Melanie took a mobile from Henry. I immediately rolled my eyes as her whole demeanor changed from the honest confident woman I knew to some sappy baby-talking bimbo. She made some excuse why she couldn't come to his great bellow. I realized they hadn't had an actual date tonight; he just needed her attention right then.

"Oh Henwy. I'll be over soon." She snapped the phone closed and glared at me.

"Isn't it presumptuous of him just to mobile you and expect you to jump at his every wish?"

"You haven't even met him yet. You don't know."

"Trust me. I know exactly how much you are changing to meet this Henry's needs." It took me everything not to change the R to a W in his name the way she did. There were others in the room and I didn't want to humiliate her. I knew it would only push her away.

"I am not."

"There is something wrong with this Mel, I can feel it."

"You mean something's wrong with him."

"No, something's wrong with you."

"Whatever! You should talk. You and Gregory might as well have a special toilet made. You two practically go to the bathroom together." She stood up not even an inch from my face.

"Girls, take a breather for a sec." Luke interjected but he couldn't get us to break eye contact.

"Please stay here with us." I begged when she turned to leave. I touched her arm and it instantly induced a vision.

He was there, a man I had never met, yet some things were familiar. It was the ten-foot tall shadow I remembered from our trip but with a different face. He had my girl, Melanie, strapped to a gurney with his eyes wild with insanity. I heard a whisper in the still air. *Soul Shifter!*

"That is a Soul Shifter. Poor Kelly. And my dream, with Great Aunt Helen. She married a Soul Shifter." I said trying to put things together.

"NO!" Melanie cried. "It can't be true. He loves me. Not another fake after it all, after the weeks I put in and the offers I refused. I could have gone out with a Cavalier. Most men lie. I can usually hear their motives and say no right away." Melanie babbled.

"But he was able to get passed your radar. That is why you are so standoffish. You let this one in and fell for him." I hugged her. "Does anyone have any more information on Soul Shifters?"

"My Abuela," Luke spoke up, "Talked about a type of Chupacabra that possessed evil doers such as rapist and murders. Their deeds are what allowed the possessions to take place. The Chupacabra could walk the earth and be one of the living and therefore affect the lives of the living."

"Pulling the ones they interact with from their set path and shifting the soul off its destiny." I finished. "Great Aunt Helen never had the children that Juniper had predicted because she married Ronny Chase."

"Nola, are there any old pictures of Juniper and maybe even the parties Helen attended to during that time period when they were friends? I need specifically parties."

"Yeah, actually there are quite a few photo albums. My father loved to take pictures. They started dating around the time the first affordable 35mm became available."

Nola left and came back with three very thick albums, each about the size of a small coffee table. She laid them out for me while the others dispersed except Mel and Gregory. I was grateful for the air space. It was getting hard to think with all of them bearing down on me all the time.

I found myself quite frustrated. Every time I turned a page, there would be one or two pictures missing with the placeholders still there. Names and dates at the bottom, but no picture in its place. Then I saw their names. Helen and Juniper at the Botanical Gardens 1925. Of course no picture above. Then I was suddenly aware what happened. Juniper in a fit of despair pulled all the pictures from the album that involves my Aunt Helen. She was unable to cope with the loss of their friendship. She needed to forget her altogether to move on and raise Nola. Even the wedding photos were pillaged. Juniper in her white gown getting her hair done up sitting on a chest. I grabbed the album staring at a group of pictures that seemed blurrier than the rest. I realized James Cross wasn't the one who took those pictures. I had a sudden red haze: James was handing Aunt Helen the camera showing her how to use it.

Then I heard, "Thanks Helen, sometimes the pictures right before the bride walks down the isle are the most prophetic."

I stared at that picture for about twenty minutes. Looking at Juniper's hair, her jewelry, the way she crossed her legs, the hem of the lace dress and her slippers that laid right in front of the sunburst carved on the side of the chest.

"Hey, that is my chest." I pointed to the people in the picture as if accusing them of stealing it.

"The picture must have been taken at Helen's house. Don't some chests from that time period have false bottoms to hide important paper and jewelry?" I looked up at Gregory and he shrugged his shoulders. "What? I saw it in a movie once. Okay, dumb idea. I just thought because of the cave-

"Yes, yes, I agree I'm just realizing that my hope chest was Aunt Helen's. I didn't think I had anything that belonged to her." I began rubbing my forehead slightly wondering when this rabbit hole was going to end. I already knew where. "We have to go to my house."

Gregory and I went alone. It was nice to have my thoughts

to myself again. I worried about Melanie and this Henry. I was glad she had come around but how did she get there in the first place? Soul Shifter or not, her whole personality changed when she talked about him. I hadn't known her that long. Maybe that was how she acted with men. I was saddened and disappointed at that realization.

As we approached the house I saw the mob out front, and Gregory did a quick u-turn. I wasn't even thinking about the number of cars that were parked down my street until I saw the mob of reporters that were on my lawn from ten houses away. We were forced to park in the lot behind my house and run through the woods.

"We are going to have to break the window to your bedroom. Don't worry, I'll have it replace tomorrow." Gregory said as he raised hand with a rock in it.

"No, I can do it." I put my hand on the glass turning it into sand. "See, much quieter."

When we approached my wooden chest, Gregory pulled up things about secret compartments using his ear clip. As he read, I cleared the stuff off the top.

"Okay, it says here that the key needs to be turned five times to unlock the drawer underneath." I had my keys out and did as he said.

"You keep the key with you?"

"I needed a place to hide my fantasy books from my mom. That is why I put so many things on top to disguise it." I heard the top click open with the first turn, which was the norm.

"She didn't put it in your room?"

"No, my dad did. That is why I didn't know it was Helen's. I've always had the chest and key in my room. I thought it was my Dad's because he gave me the key." The key made its fifth turn and a triangle-hinged drawer open down revealing a small manuscript book inside and an octagon shape piece of gold.

"Helen and Juniper's Limericks 1917." Gregory read the top of the first title page and a loose page fell to the floor. I picked it up looking at the strange calligraphy.

*When I was a young lass of seventeen*
*I met a young boy and he liked me*
*We went for walks*
*Had many good talks*
*But in the end it couldn't be*
*When I was a mother at thirty-two*
*I did everything I could do*
*To make a good home*
*With the love shown*
*But they all left when they grew*

*Finally I'm now sixty-five*
*The trials a woman sees and survives*
*A man's milk would sour*
*Killing him the next hour*
*As I'd roll my eyes with a sigh*

"Well that's not very nice. I think my great grandmother just called me stupid." Gregory said raising his eyebrow.

"You should see some of the things I wrote about you when we first met but that's beside the point. There are the numbers we need."

"What with the piece of gold?"

"I'm not sure yet." I couldn't mention Lily.

"We'll have to find out later. Come on." With that he grabbed my hand and pulled me to the Vapor.

I looked out the window trying to see the amount of people that were out there on my front lawn. There had to be fifty at least, and they weren't all reporters either, some were sick in wheelchairs.

"Delia, get away from the window. Someone might see you."

"There are people out there, waiting for a miracle, who think I can help them. I can't heal all of them."

"You aren't going to even attempt one. Come on, let's go."

"Hey, I saw movement, someone's in there." One of the outsiders yelled and the doorbell started to ring.

We went back to my bedroom window and someone was coming through the broken opening. The crowd was surrounding my house now.

"Screw it." Gregory said as he grabbed my hand, pulling me through the back kitchen door. I plowed through the people charging past. That is, until my hand slipped from his. I reached forward into the sea of people searching to reconnect and a hand took mine hauling forward me again, but this time in a different direction.

I could hear Gregory's voice, "Step back and part the way", he commanded.

I thought it strange how the sound of his voice came from behind me. Then I heard him call my name.

*Who was holding my hand?*

All the people were so tight. With the confusion, I couldn't see who was pulling me. I struggled to be freed and go back to Gregory.

"Over here Delia," said a familiar voice.

"Melanie, how did you get here?" I said surprised.

"I used my Vapor silly."

"How did you get here? Wait, where is Gregory?"

"Come over this way, my Vapor is over here. Gregory has been looking for you. Come on, over here."

She was pulling me, rushing to avoid the swallowing crowd that was now grabbing at me. Before I knew, it she was shoving me into a Vapor that wasn't hers. It was black.

"Mel, what's going on? Where is Gregory?" The inside

was very dark and I felt someone covering my mouth with a smelly cloth and everything went black.

When I woke I was very cold and strapped to a gurney. Melanie came over to me, she began brushing the hair from my eyes.

"It's going to be okay, Delia. He is here to help us."

"Mel, please untie me." I struggled.

"Sorry, you can't be trusted with those magic hands of yours." Mel smiled a funny smile.

"Who is going to help us?"

"My Henry, of course. I told him I was a telepath. He said he can quiet the voices. He can help you too and make the pain go away. Won't it be great never to feel anyone else's emotions but your own?"

Melanie was acting like a bimbo again. It must be some sort of effect he had on her. I immediately forgave her treachery; she couldn't help the power he had over her.

"Where am I?" I asked quickly.

"A warehouse on Chester. Oops, probably shouldn't have said that." Whatever Henry had done to her had made her ditzy.

"No, you shouldn't have my darling, but I don't think it's going to matter." A man approached from the corner. It was the coldness in his voice that made my skin crawl.

"Hello Delia, you remember me don't you? Well maybe not exactly this body. You can recognize the entity from within. I suppose that would be one of your 'gifts' as you call them."

"Yes, I am able to see you."

"Well then let me inform you how very special you are, you're the only one who has ever. All this time the great and wonderful human race has never acknowledged that we exist when you're the ones who created us. Your ancestor Helen Bracken had no clue, even when she married me."

"You were Ronny Chase."

"My dear, I have had many names. I had a hard time

coming up with a way to tear Juniper and Helen's friendship apart. Until I stumbled on the torso killer and influenced him to bump into Helen that one day. That is what it took, a vision of a young girl being killed to get her to come to my side and then she didn't want her psychic ability anymore."

"Why would you want to mess up Helen's destiny?"

"The child she was supposed to have was to be very important. I couldn't let her meet her mate, the one who would marry her. Unfortunately, you found a way to be born. The important ones always do." He frowned.

"What are you talking about?" I bit my lip.

"You, Delia. It has always been about you, finding your way to change the world. We Soul Shifters like the world the way it is. If the humans ascend then where will we be? We won't be able to follow them there. We are their doubts and fears. If you show them what you can do then, we will cease to exist. I wish I could kill you but there will end up being another. That is why I have found a way to cryogenically freeze you. Your cousin was so useful; her daddy was able to get me all the funding I needed at his university. All it took was a little push from me."

"They all think you're dead."

"Doug Walsh is dead. I had to change bodies. His midnight escapades were catching up with him. You should thank me, I saved your cousin's life by not letting him kill her."

"What is going to happen, um, Henry, is it?"

This was great. I was getting all the answers I needed. The bad guys always talk too much bragging about their greatness. That is always their downfall.

"Yes. I suppose Henry will be just fine. Now it is time for your injections. I really hope they hurt. You have been such a pain in our ass."

He came over and shoved a very big syringe into my arm and yeah it hurt. I was focusing on his bright shiny light that I wanted to grab. My ARMS that were tied down were restricted. If I could just bend my elbow, I thought. I could see Melanie heard my thoughts.

*It will help Melanie if I could touch him. I want to help. I understand now. He left the room to get something else. Untie me Melanie, I want the pain to go away.*

She walked over and loosened the straps. I had the sudden concern that Melanie was permanently damaged. I needed to know she was going to be all right before I took care of Henry.

"What have you done to her?" I accused him when he came back because it was obvious she wasn't acting of her own free will.

"She is a telepath making her very susceptible to my influence more than normal. Unfortunately, it turned her brain to mush and she isn't as useful to me as a human."

"Why do you keep acting like me and Melanie aren't human?"

"How else would you have your ability?" Henry laughed. "Your DNA is different because your ancestors weren't from here. Always meddling, your kind was. Trying to save those stupid bags of bones."

"Will Melanie be okay?"

"Why would I know to care? I'm planning on leaving her here with your frozen body to drool all over herself until she expires, like groceries do."

"You're planning on leaving me behind."

"Well I very well can't take you with me," Henry spat.

"Can't I just be defrosted?"

"You see that is the great thing. There is no known technology to reanimate, only to sustain life so the cells aren't damaged during the freezing process. You should feel honored. Many Arctic ground squirrels gave their lives so that I could make you this little cocktail. Bottoms up baby."

With that he injected the next round. The pain made me cry Gregory's name and then I was standing in front of Gregory at the Cross House.

"Delia? Where are you?" Gregory cried.

"I can't tell you. He's too dangerous. He has the ability to influence the way you do, but worse. With Soul Shifters there is no free will."

"You tell me now. Where are you? Let me protect you."

"You can't, Sweets. I am going to finish this one on my own." I blew him a kiss.

"He must be hurting you or you wouldn't have contacted me. You are obviously in pain. Let us help you. Please Delia." Tears were streaming down Gregory's face.

"I love you, Gregory." With that, I broke the connection.

"Did you take a little trip, Delia?" The Soul Shifters face hover above mine, his breath smelled like rotten flesh. "Your powers have no effect on me. You can't break this body. It was already dead the minute I entered it."

"I have something to tell you." I whispered.

"What would that be, a last request? Are you going to beg? You don't seem the type really."

"You know even the most evil entities have souls?"

"Anything created has a soul," he growled.

"So you admit you have a soul."

"Yes. That is how I take over a body. I replace the soul with mine, only I splinter it." That was why I could see its soul. It was splintered. Never having a path to follow causing chaos.

"Do you want to know my favorite gift?" I coughed.

"Oh, please indulge me before I silence that pretty mouth for all eternity." He held the final injection up looking at it. "Tell me quickly. I only have the crystallizing protein left and you won't be able to talk or move anymore after this one."

"I bring peace to chaos." With that I pulled out of my bindings and yanked his soul from his body. Holding it in my hand I watched it blink.

"What are you doing to Henry?" Melanie asked mechanically.

*Helping him*, I thought.

Thinking seemed to penetrate louder than voice, controlling her mentally because that was how her gift worked. She backed up, letting me sit up. I arranged his soul so not one splinter was left, then placed it back into the body. I was afraid what I did wouldn't work. I couldn't put the soul anywhere else; it boomeranged right into its place.

"What was I doing?" As before it was if he could see right through me. I didn't exist anymore and was protected.

"Henrwy?" Melanie whined.

"Who are you?" He asked, looking to Mel.

*Melanie, tell him he is late and needs to turn himself into the police for whatever he has done. Tell him it will be fun.*

She did as I told her and he was gone. He was just as easy to control as Melanie. Now if I could only reverse the process.

*Melanie, come here.*

She was next to me and I placed my hands on the side of her head touching her forehead to mine. I let my life energy flow into her openly.

*Melanie, come back. Please come back.*

*Then my body was shaking and everything faded to black.*

# CHAPTER 17

The room was blurry and I could hear familiar voices. Nola, Melanie and Miranda were in the room awaiting my next instructions. Good, they got the message I sent them. Nola and Miranda knew when I would wake up and got rid of Gregory so we could talk without interruption.

"Are you back with us then my darling?" Nola asked.

"Uh huh." I grumbled coming from my dream state. 'Melanie, are you okay?' I thought.

"Of course I'm okay. What a crazy question considering your current situation!" Melanie squeaked.

*I'll be fine just give me a minute.*

Yes, and I could feel my legs this time. Now I needed to get my tongue to work.

*Luke, I need him.* Melanie continued to translate my grunts.

"I sent the boys out on an errand. I thought it might look a little suspicious if I just sent Greggy out by himself. Don't worry, Luke and Phineas have been updated. It was much easier getting Gregory out of the house with those two on board.

"How long?

There was this weird silence and they all looked at each other as if passing the buck mentally. I addressed Melanie to focus an answer. I needed to plan our next action.

*MELANIE, WHAT DAY IS IT?*

I screamed at her from my thoughts.

"Geez, Delia," Melanie put her hands over her ears. "You don't have to yell. It's like feedback from a microphone when you do that and it echoes, reverberating against my skull."

*Sorry, but I need to know.*

"It is 5:30 in the evening on July 6th." Nola spoke up while placing a hand on my cheek.

"WHAT!" I found my voice on my own. Sitting up, I turn my body to get out of bed.

"Calm down Delia," Miranda said.

"But I have so little time to prepare." The three shared that look again.

"We have been thinking, well hoping, you wouldn't go through with this." Miranda's eyes filled up with tears. She didn't want to lose another daughter. I was honored she thought of me as family.

"There is no way to know for sure what will happen. The point is to keep Gregory away from me when it is happening." I took Miranda's hand trying to ease her fear.

"Well, what was in the vault? No…screw that." I got myself out of bed and started walking down the hallway taking the elevator to the second floor.

Approaching the secret elevator, the nerves in my throat hoped the resources would be down there. Great Aunt Helen's instructions were to a tee but would be meaningless without the proper equipment. Melanie rushed ahead with the limerick in hand to unlock the vault.

The vault was smaller than I imagined. It was about the size of a narrow half bathroom. Along the wall were about a hundred writing journals.

"Hey are those-"

"Helen and my mother's journals in perfect order. Each page or entry has a prediction on it. Miranda and I have read them all, looking for a clue on how to get you out of this mess. I'm afraid we are at a loss. Most of the predictions are events that have already taken place. Except for the constant theme of a magnetic change in July of this year. There is not a word of those Soul Shifters."

"Helen and Juniper had no idea something of such great evil existed or that it could destroy their friendship." I shivered thinking of Aunt Helen sleeping next to Ronny Chase. "She deserved better than that snake. I wish I could make it all right for her and the only way I know is to finish this."

"Even if you die." Melanie was shaking.

"Yes Mel, even if I die. My soul has to be released to cleanse the negative energy. I'm not sure I'll be able to just pop back inside my body right after."

"I thought you weren't sure about what the end game holds." Melanie frowned.

"You can't protect me and you must not interfere in the process whatever is supposed to happen."

"I'm so sorry," Nola whispered. "There are others you know, others that will come after you if you choose not to do this. We read in the journals there have been many before, some who have succeeded and some who have not. Every five hundred years to be exact. The worst that will happen is you will be left out of the Philosophy books of the future. Please, my Greggy can't take another loss of this magnitude and neither can the rest of us." She begged me.

"You're wrong, Nola. You know nothing of the Soul Shifters; they get stronger everyday. If things get much worse, I don't think we will be able to ascend to the next plane." Nola opened her mouth to protest, but I continued softly, "Where is the clock?"

There were those blanks stares again, hiding something from me. They thought I wouldn't know about the clock. It was the proof negating all arguments to keep me from my mission. It told the truth they were ignoring. This was our last chance to be put on the track to enlightenment. All those books talking about how something or someone takes the good and leaves the bad weren't true. We won't be going anywhere if we don't start pulling our weight as a group together. In one solid positive force, we could move on. I was their symbol screaming tick-tock it's the souls time, get off your asses and on your path. This was the shock needed to balance happiness and responsibility.

"The clock please?" I asked one more time.

Reluctantly the three parted looking forlorn. Melanie pulled off a white slipcover revealing something half the size of a Vapor. Although it had a face of a clock, the intricate detail on its wooden and brass frame was unmistakable. Below the sixth hour was an additional half dial with strange words pointing to the far right.

"What language is that?" I asked not sure.

"Luke said it is a dead language he doesn't know."

Again, with the side glances! They weren't lying, my empath ability told me, but they were holding something back. Then I had flash of a vision telling me what I wanted to know.

"But the journals did tell you, Juniper loved research. I'm sure once she found the clock, she also had to know what those words meant."

Even though I knew this, I needed them to face the reality. This was bigger than all of us and they couldn't save me.

"Its dial points to the far right and the phrase above translates into Burdened Hearts as in the whole world's sadness because of the negativity that has been created. There is so much confusion on what a person has to accomplish he/she cannot see their path. We have more to entertain us theses days. It fills our heads, occupying the mind, no one can see the importance of listening to the spirit within." Melanie said rubbing her head. My thoughts were too much for her. I could feel her headache coming on.

"Do you want your children, grandchildren and great grandchildren to live with this and struggle with it themselves?"

I looked at each face, knowing I had hit the mark. So I added, "You all have to help me. It is the reason why you are standing here."

"I guess that means I'm part of this Alignment thing." Melanie tried to lighten the mood with her own resolve.

"Only if you want to be. You have a choice. Everyone has free will."

"Unless you are dating a soul shifter." Melanie made fun.

I look at her about to defend her from herself and she continued with, "I know I'm special with my telepathic ability that makes me more susceptible. Blah blah. I will do anything I can to stop those bastards. You doing this will kill them, right?"

"There will always be evil. Humans created it and controlled how much power it has over their lives. I think what I'm about to do is create a symbol that will generate a type of cleansing that makes room for hope. For Hopeful Hearts?" I asked the three women.

"For Hopeful Hearts." Melanie responded quickly.

"For Hopeful Hearts." Nola nodded solemnly.

"Gregory already hates me and this will seal it for life," Miranda began, "but what I'm worried is he will never forgive you. He'll hate you Delia." Miranda approached me standing close.

"He will find another to love and her work will be just as important." I felt the tears coming and shoved them away.

"Your sacrifice is to be admired. He may hate me, but I will not let him forget how much you truly love him. For Hopeful Hearts." Miranda finished the pack. With that she hugged me kissing the top of my head and tucking it under her chin as if I was her infant. She was making a memory and reliving one at the same time, thinking of Lily.

I had them on my side and that would be enough to sway Phin and Luke. In truth Phin could care less about me, wanting to go back to his life was his goal no matter how much he and Gregory were getting along now. Luke was another story and a short one. He would follow me off a bridge because that was who he was. He trusted his heart and he knew I was doing what needed to be done. Although I think I will leave out the part about me dying. He knew most of it any way.

I couldn't tell them all together or Gregory would suspect something. I decided to lie back down while Nola prepared dinner and I wanted to appear frail to Gregory. He couldn't know I was up to something. If I pretended to be sick than just maybe he couldn't tell I was lying through my teeth to him. He knew me too well and I really had to pull out all the stops. No matter how much it hurt, and it did hurt. Our connection was strong, I felt an actual physical pain in my heart. I was being torn from him by distancing myself. I hoped he couldn't feel it too. Playing sick was the only thing there was to disguise my betrayal.

"Hey, Grandma said you wouldn't be up for hours." Gregory said as he came in. "I wouldn't have gone out if I'd known." He laid next to me his face in mine sharing my pillow. I looked into his eyes so bright with promise. I was unable to speak and tears started to fall.

"My love, is this about tomorrow?" I nodded my head yes. "You shouldn't worry everything will work out. The important thing is we'll be together through it all."

I opened my mouth to speak and nothing could come. "Can't talk? Don't be embarrassed? Luke will have you speaking in no time. How are the legs? Are you able to walk?"

I wiggled my toes slightly and lift each leg. "Good! Come, Nola's making your favorite dinner."

After dinner I sat by the fire in the parlor watching the flames dance. All the women talked about nonsense and their fear was building up inside me. Luke came behind me and rubbed my back. He wasn't afraid, neither was Phin or Gregory. They were my stone pillars balancing the energy. Where the women feared for me, the men believed in me.

They really didn't know someone was going to die, but I was sure of it.

Luke bent down to my ear whispering,
"When should I do it?"

"I'll nod to you when to act."

"He's going to put up a struggle and it will hurt him.

"That's fine," I sighed."You do realize you're betraying him. I can go through with it, no problem, but can you?"

"Yes. I won't be worrying about Gregory's pain levels." I stood up to go up for bed.

Gregory walked me to my room but I pulled him on past it to one of the vacant guest rooms. Earlier I had taken the dust cover off the bed and put on clean sheets.

"What are you doing?" Gregory asked as I took off my clothes. I ignored him.

I was completely naked before him when I said, "Take your clothes off, Gregory." This time he was deaf, staring down from my breasts to my more delicate area.

"Delia we can't." He said wincing.
His face read pain but his body was rushing with desire. He slammed his hands into his pockets and closed his eyes slowly backing away. Making me rush up to him before he could reach the door.

"Run rabbit run." I said softly.

I began to unbutton his shirt.

"Please stop." His voice was weak and images of his desire filled my mind.

"Yes, I would like that too." I whispered. He stepped back clearing his throat he then commanded,

"Delia, I want you to put your clothes back on."

I could only smile. "You have no power here, my Gregory. I know what I want and what I want is you." With that I hugged his bare chest stroking my lips with his. He couldn't resist securing me to him and automatically my legs wrapped around his waist. It was then his mind entered into mine I had become nervous. I lost my resolve and he knew it.

"Step back, my love." I released him and did as I was told.

"No," I whispered begging him, "Please Gregory I want this."

"I have stated before, Delia, it is not your wants I care about. It is only your needs that concern me. You need love, but what you ask of me isn't love, it is mating."

"You have no idea how ridiculous you sound." I said irritated.

"Think about it Delia-"

"I don't want to think, I want to do." I cried out. The rejection was becoming too much.

"Exactly, my love. You aren't being rational or we would be on that bed by now. It is only when you are ready we will become one and you will have your way with me."

I was going to die a virgin and he couldn't know it. I couldn't tell him. My anger was building and I wanted to break something or possibly someone. My body was on fire with my brain targeting the source, and this time it was Gregory.

# CHAPTER 18

Gregory started coming towards me and I put a hand out stopping him. As my palm faced him I accidentally fired my rage and threw him back. His mouth slammed against the bedpost and was bleeding.

Seeing the horror in my eyes he said, "It's okay, Sweets, I'm alright."

All I could think was how thick everything around me seemed. The room swelled as the tears burst from my eyes. I almost killed him. Thoughts of Gregory dead flashed through my mind.

Running from the room, I heard Gregory call for me. Finally making my way outside the house, I began to cry, mourning the life we were meant to have together. Maybe it was a fitting end; my demise tomorrow was the equivalent of putting down a rabid dog.

"Why do you ask this of me?" I scream when I reach the beach. "Why can't I have a little piece of him to take with me? Tell him I'm ready!" I raved, pointing at the sky.

I was surrounded by the sounds of nature and nothing else; the wind brought no answers or visions. I laid down feeling the sand below my body grabbing handfuls letting it slide between my fingers knowing I would be a part of it tomorrow. Sitting up hugging my legs, I cried and cried. Footsteps hushed my whimpers, but I could not cease the rocking motion.

"Go away Phin, I'm naked." The anger had taken my modesty and what I wanted was to embarrass him hoping he'd leave.

"You're not my type, a little fat in the rear if you ask me."

"Go the hell away!"

"I'm here to look at the drones. Ugh, are they lovely. You leave."

"I was here first."

"No you weren't. I'm pretty sure 'the first' was some Native American."

"Whatever stay, just shut up."

"Wow such transference. I'm not the one you tried to seduce. Don't blame me because you were unsuccessful."

"I hate you. In fact I hate you so much I've decide I don't want your help. I release you. There, you got what you want. GO!" I stood up facing him.

"Yeah, funny thing about hate. Passion has a lot to do with it. I knew you always wanted me."

"Don't act like you understand me. I could have killed him and I want to hurt you right now. I have evil inside me and it's waiting to strike."

"As usual, you're wrong. I hope you're not wrong about something tomorrow. Messing up world peace would be a bummer."

"Get away from me." I yelled.

"Nope, I'm in the mood and it's fun. Too bad my son didn't have the balls to do it. All that fire would have been hot."

I snapped. The same as I had with Gregory, I shoved Phin into the bushes next to the stairs. He got up dusting himself off and I threw him back again. He came again and I shoved him into the sand, next into the cement rocks. He came again and again until I was tired and collapsed to my knees, gasping for air as I was suddenly out of breath.

I closed my eyes to focus on my breathing, bringing me back to when I was in yoga class with Gregory. I then felt a coat covering my shoulders and there was Phin, helping me to stand back up to my feet.

"You think you're evil and can't control yourself," he started as he buttoned up the trench coat. "You could have thrown me into the rocks or the stairs. But you were careful just as you tried to throw Gregory on the bed. It was his fault he flailed and smacked his mouth on the post. Delia you aren't evil, even subconsciously." He picked me up to carry me into the house.

"How much do you love Gregory?" I asked Phin on the way up the stairs.

"Enough to hurt him."

"That's all I need to know."

"Good. I'm getting tired of counseling the leader of this group." Phin's smartass way of saying he was behind me.

"Wait, Phin. What are the five golden rings?"

Phin put me down. "They are my life's work. I have four out of five. The rest are in safety deposit in a bank downtown. No one knows, but me."

"What are they?"

They are from our alien ancestors. They were given as presents to their new human wives or husbands. They got the idea from watching penguins."

"How do you know about this?"

"My father told me before he died."

"What are they for?"

"I don't know. My dad told me it was our family's job and it was important." Phin shrugged.

"Can you go get them?"

"Yes. Why and how do you know about this?"

"Lily told me."

"I'll go and get them right now."

Inside everyone wanted to talk. Phin did the most honorable thing I ever seen him do for me. He got everyone to shut up. He used their thoughts against them by twisting each of their thoughts so they where red with embarrassment. This was a shocker for Melanie. She had everyone invading her thoughts and purity was all she knew. Phin knew the intention of every thought; she never tried to use it to hurt someone. She had so many balls she juggled; to be able to decode every thought that wandered into her head was impossible. Phin got to pick and choose what he absorbed.

I found Gregory blockading my door, holding his lip with an ice pack.

"I just want to go to bed." I said glaring at him.

"Is there something you're not telling me?"

"If you mean that you might be a major jerk, then I guess we've cleared the air."

"You know I can make you tell me." My heart sped up. Crap, that had never occurred to me. No. No. I'd better calm down, stand straight, hold my head up and get right in his face.

"Who do you think you're talking to? I am the leader and if I have held something back then maybe it's for the best. You wouldn't want Nola dying because you messed things up, would you?" And there it was, my ability to lie. Lie with a partial truth and you can own anyone. Even someone you love.

"Grand-ma?" he stuttered. Nola was his only connection to a parent, the only one that counted to him. Miranda and Phin had yet to earn that back.

"Yes. Nola." Every word felt evil coming from me. His fear confirmed I was on the right track. I had to make sure not to touch him. If I absorbed his fear he'd be able to clear his head and make me talk.

"How do you know this?"

"I know everything including the stupid thing you do to get her killed."

"I kill Nola. How can we prevent this?"

"Listen to my exact instruction and do not act impulsively when we are out there tomorrow. You must stand behind her not in front. When we are finished, you lose your balance and accidentally push her from the pier."

"Why would something horrible like that happen after we've created so much good?"

"Because, Gregory, there no guaranteed contracts in life. Just because I do this then I should automatically get that. It doesn't work that way as you have taught me tonight." With that stunning him I ran around him and slammed the door, locking it. I didn't want him coming in the middle of the night. I needed rest and he could make me fold with more pushing.

I awoke early the next morning hoping they all slept sound. I went down to the vault taking the cover from the clock. Placing my hands on the bottom of its stand, sad I would be destroying such a beautiful antique but I knew there was no other way. The clocks exterior was carved from a solid piece of wood, there were no gaps screw or glue. I carefully obliterated the front hoping maybe it could one day be repaired. Below the mechanism was a single silver tube, at least that is how I would have described it if Aunt Helen hadn't have told me.

"I hold in my hand the weapon that will change the world and kill me." I said out loud, dusting it off using my robe.

"You are not alone in this my dear." Nola surprised me from behind.

"Remember what you said the first day we found out I was psychic? You said heaven and earth would one day be the same plane. Will I even make it to heaven with my soul in pieces? Will I exist at all to see the two planes unite?"

"I don't know. I wouldn't have pushed you if I knew your true purpose."

"I would have been miserable. Isn't that how it works? You're not happy unless you're walking your path, unless you're doing something you are passionate about."

"Yes, but it's not fair."

I shrugged. "At least I got to meet my true love."

Phin showed up, breathing hard. "Here they are."

I arranged all the pieces on the floor. They felt funny to the touch. Like there was energy in them. I was trying to figure out how to connect them together when they moved all by themselves, coming together, forming a circle about the size of my hand.

"Holy shit," Phin cried. His life's work right in front of him.

"Thank you," I picked it up protectively.

"Come to my room. I have something to show you." Nola whispered.

We walked up to Nola's room where her bed had a beautiful white dress with billowing sleeves and pearls embroidering the neckline. I stood there awhile until I got up the nerve to touch it. I didn't want to see my own death.

"It's yours." She said and she nudged me forward.

"I know," was all I could come up with.

I laid my fingers upon it thinking I'd see death, hear screaming and feel the pain of my spirit being blown apart into a zillion pieces, instead I heard laughter and felt bliss and I remembered something Aunt Helen had told me in my slumbers. I was not giving death to the world but a helping hand to happiness. How could I deny Gregory that…how could I deny the world that?

With conviction I put the dress on ready for my fate. The gauntlet slipped on my upper arm and wrist secured around my thumb and four fingers. The markings on it were symbols and I realized they were Egyptian. I placed the gold circle in the forearm of it. I knew what would happen if I made a fist and didn't want risk damaging it. I decide to wait until the time was right. When I put my arms to my side the billowing sleeves were perfect to hide the silver antique from the one person who loved me the most and stood in the way of my destiny.

Exiting Nola's room, I saw him looking gorgeous and perfect. I ran up to him and kissed him as hard as I could, making a memory and knowing it was our final kiss. I hugged him with my one free arm, the other held dead at my side with gauntlet.

"I love you," I whispered breathless.

"I guess that would mean you're not mad at me any longer." He smirked.

"Don't be so sure of yourself Superman." I patted his chest and looked at the grandfather clock on the hall: less than one hour left.

"Hey, we need to tal-"

"DONG," the doorbell rang as the grandfather clock chimed interrupting our last private conversation together. I heard a familiar high-pitched voice from the foyer.

"The Little Press is here," Luke joked.

"Where'd you put your uniform nursey? Is it right next to your panty drawer?" Manny Spada barked.

"Manny, I'm sorry but I'm running out of time here. As you can see, I have an event I'm attending," referencing the dress I was wearing as it being important.

"I have some questions for you. There has been a development that must be addressed."

"Why are you here, Manny?" I sighed.

"I have something to show you." He held up a DVD and then tossed it to Gregory. "Here put this on, Sasquatch." We went into the Media Room and Gregory did as he was told but I read severe animosity on his face. The interview I did with Manny popped up on the flat screen.

"Okay, what is so different?" I said in a rushed voice.

"Well it took me a second to figure it out too. Just wait."

The interview we did together started with Manny's voice dubbed over in Spanish then with my part came up answering a question I was talking like I always do in English.

"So what?" I asked impatiently.

"Do you know how many times we have tried to dub over your voice with another language, any language and couldn't?"

"Okay." I folded my arms. I needed him to get to the point.

"We talked to other networks, Delia, and they all have the same problem. Until we asked those who weren't bilingual and they understood your part of the interview perfectly. The dubbing wasn't necessary for you. Your words are your own and remained unchanged."

"Is anyone understanding what this worm is getting at?" Gregory crossed his arms.

"How is it possible?" Manny said with exasperation and I looked at Luke.

"Some of us have gifts other than healing."

"Wait! I have to get this." He ran to the door and brought out his viewer. "This will go straight to a live feed if I want."

Gregory looked out the window. "Are those your three shuttles out there?"

"Three?" Manny ran to the window.
"Crap, I was followed."

Reporters emerged from their trucks with their camera guys. Then I saw the people start to appear, it was the sick and the suffering. The doorbell rang and I jumped, but I didn't turn from the window because I saw them, not one, not ten but too many to count Soul Shifters, appearing one by one. They came toward the window. One threw a rock, shattering the glass before me. This frightened the people causing them to back off.

"I will kill you. I'll kill you all." I screamed through the broken glass but my brain began targeting everything, including the people. I would do anything to complete my task now even if it meant killing a few to save the bunch.

"Delia," Gregory held me close. "We must run to the vault to figure out the rest of the Prophecy."

"I know the rest, you fool." I wasn't in control anymore. The warrior was taking over.

"What must we do then my love?" Gregory asked in his

charming voice.

"Go down to the beach." I said and I began to walk forward through the window.

"NO," Gregory raised his voice and then thought about it. Then I turned at him. "It would be best to go down the way of the vault."

"Yes, the vault."

"What the hell is wrong with her?" Manny said with fear.

"Her spirit is taking over and preparing for its task." Gregory said to Manny holding his camera, not even realizing it was on. "Just don't get in her way."

We went up and then down again in the elevator, as Manny came up with question after question, which Melanie answered quickly and quietly. It took two trips for all of us to make it down. When we all made it too the bottom, we heard the Soul Shifters break through the front door. Gregory disabled the elevator at the bottom. Then every one's cell went off.

They all said simultaneously, "We have five minutes."

We ran down the corridor, out the steel door, and around the waterfall to the stone pier. The stones were cold after running through the warm sand. When I reached the end, I turned to see a line of Soul Shifters on the cliffs above and some began to descend down those crumbly old steps.

"What happens now?" Gregory said.
"You have to hurry! They're coming." Phin yelled, quickly placing himself behind Gregory and in front of Luke.

"An act of love and betrayal, sorry but I can't have another bed post experience happening right now" I said as Phin removed a piece of already cut duct tape from his pant leg. Luke kicked out his knees and then grabbed Gregory's hands securing them behind his body while Phin placed the tape over his mouth. The two held him kneeling in place while a very confused Gregory mumbled "Delia no!" through the tape the best that he could.

I could hear him desperately fighting to free himself while Luke and Phin help keep the restraints. Drowning out Gregory's pleas became easier, my ear was tingly from what I guessed to be the ear clip's alien like countdown. A series of frequencies ringing in unison that produce one solid vibration. A beat that resembles that the heart, with each beat louder and louder, I feel the coarse of vibrations its creating through my body, right down to my cellular structure.

Three Soul Shifters had made their way to the end of the pier and were now running faster towards us. It's at this moment the ear clip's vibrations are synced up with my own heartbeat, the coarse of adrenaline so strong it visualizes a pulsing aura like force field for all to see. And apparently it also works like a steel close-line as the three approaching Soul Shifters are halted by their throats and shoulders, being thrown into the ground with extreme force.

Looking forward past their fallen horizon I can see swarms of drones by the thousand getting ready to enter the dome. The clouds have created a storms eye above my head, as if commanding me, I pointed my arm straight up and made a fist. A very long silver rod descended from the gauntlet. The realization of what was about to happen hit Gregory and he struggled harder to free himself. Standing all of four feet behind him were two familiar auras, "Lily and my Dad, is that you?" *Great timing! I think that's them, their souls watching me, I can use all the support I can get right now.*

"Remember my love," I yelled back to Gregory as the wind picked up wildly. "Even death won't keep me from you."

At this very point a bolt of lighting released from the storm's eye, surging directly into the gauntlet's silver rod. A heat so hot and bright, it pierced my soul in unison to stabbing the ear clip's last beat. The bolt of lighting became a flowing golden energy beam coursing a comfortable warmth. Time slowed so much it felt frozen, I was different, entirely different as I look down to see myself dead. With only my solid soul radiating, my standing presences remains. Glowing sand became my entity. Pulling my new hand closer to my face I observe the tiny glowing particles, I can almost see microscopic versions of myself. Something is telling me my soul is infinite? At that moment an instinct I've never felt before told me to release time I must let myself go. Drones are now floating downward from the sky like ash remains from a comet. With electronics, the pulsating energy from my aura's force field struck them all, like a battery taken to steel wool, I was watching a death metal borealis. That's not the same with Soul Shifters and the human body. Observing the entire playing field now, I can see everyone I love about to meet their death.

*If I don't act they could kill everyone I love.* Manny, Nola, Melanie, Miranda, Luke, Phin, my dear Gregory the more I thought of them the stronger my energy field grew. Hearing their cries made the sand from the beach raise and twirl around my particle self, elevating me towards the storm's eye like a kettle releasing it's steam of rage.

I looked up as the Soul Shifters were five feet from Manny. I saw the white brilliance of it all. The hotness and bone rattling rawness of our souls. Each and everyone of us like a star belonging to the galaxy, but graced over the terrain of earth. A glow so great, so magnificent I would give every last bit of myself for its existence to belong to us. Noticing Lily and my dad transition their spirits into eagles, I can see one of Lily's talons free Gregory's hands from his bounds.

Worried about Manny I can already see one Soul Shifter take Miranda by the hair. Another had picked Nola up by her face, throwing her a good fifteen feet towards a now free Gregory. The more pain I witnessed the more I began to grow. Figuring out how to turn particles of sand into myself became as easy as breathing. The now trillion upon trillions of pieces that made me felt light as a feather.

I directed a scream of hate as I pointed at the Soul

Shifter trying to consume Melanie. Before I knew it my arm looked like it was a glowing tube shooting sand that twirled around to engulf the Soul Shifter. *So this is how it's done, how far I can spread myself across this earth. It has to do with love, the love for this entire planet and its future.* I brought both of my fists close to my stomach, inhaling enough air to let out one last burst of energy. The beam of energy that connected me to the Storm's eye became thick as a skyscraper with my last scream so loud it vibrated the oceans.

As my soul transformed into small grains of sand covering every inch of the world, absorbing the negativity from the invading Soul Shifters, filtering it through myself until I could taste dirt, and hear the roots of trees they were okay. I was becoming one with earth. I could feel the energy field from the storm's eye letting go. What was once a beam of light that shot up into space was now just a struggling laser pointer.

Hope is not lost, Lily and my dad a circling over me, with their spirit talons were able to catch enough of my soul's essence for rejuvenation. Seeing my body in Gregory's arms laying there I desperately reach out. Somehow Gregory knew to hold up my dead body's hand, that's was the only way I could grab the remaining essence with both my spirit hand and real hand together.

"Come back to me!" I heard his voice call for me.

"I can't," I called back from the dark.

"Damn it, Delia. You get back into your body, you stupid girl!"

"My body is dead and my spirit is everywhere."

"Come back! NOW!" He screamed.

"It's so dark. I don't know the way." I reached for his mind and I could see through his eyes, my lifeless body in his arms. He took my hands and put them on my chest.

"Are you telling me you can heal everyone in this world and not yourself? You're not leaving me. You come back into your body and I want every last morsel of you back. Your

MIND, BODY and SOUL COME BACK TO ME NOW!"
He commanded and my spirit ignited pulling itself back into
my body. "Please! I love you! Heal yourself! Heal yourself!
Listen to my voice!" He commanded over again. My eyes
opened for an instant to see his face and then there was nothing
but blackness. He was shaking me while hugging my arms in
place. There was a tingly in my fingers my brain
did that thing where it fogs up and I get dizzy. I hated his
powers and they annoyed me every time. My hands became hot
and my body jerked.

"There you go…and you thought I had no part in this.
I showed you." He was purposely making me angry. When I
woke up from the upcoming coma that would heal my body, he
was going to get an ear full.

I woke up sometime later from my deep sleep and all of
us continued to live our lives. We had quite a mess to clean up.
Our country itself didn't survive in the end. Everyone kind of
dispersed everywhere. Eager get to know new things. Able to
now see what other countries were like outside of our own.
Thankfully they welcomed us. Something I never knew before
like culture awareness or even simple things like the taste of a
macadamia nut are all pieces that connect us.

As far as our little group, we would come back to that
old house on the cliff at the edge of the park every once in
awhile. We'd tell our kids on the pier what happened and what
they should watch out for in the future.

I was taught to fear the stars…and now our children
were taught of the their brilliance. In fact, my children were
taught to explore the stars, to know about the alien race and
virus and how I did my best to overcome it so earth could be
protected and passed down to them.

Unfortunately, as my ancestors had to fight, I had to
fight, it may very well be a future problem for my children.
Maybe even on another planet, but a group of my descendants
are waiting for the children of the alignment to be born again,

as long as the soul shifters still continue. The evil that controls our souls only wins when we let it in, by cracking it like a whip when we harm others. Until we stop hurting one another the cycle continues within us all. Progress will always have its struggles. Life's solution, its purest existence is love.

That's peace. Whether or not if it came before or after war, it's something that remains an infinite cycle to life. Earth will always have it's battles, it's mysteries, it's galaxy. It will always hold life, it will always offer love.

We just have to be smart enough to accept it and give. That's what any parent wants for their children...to give a world and life their children can love, grow, and be a part of its existence.

How will you pursue yours?